# 1e Genesis 6 Project

## Michael Ferguson

Shock Rock Publishing

Copyright © 2022 by Michael Ferguson

Cover design by Mark Reid and Author Package

Maps © 2022 T E Shepherd Art & Illustration. All rights reserved

Shock Rock Publishing

Established 2022

Shock Rock Publishing Original, Printing 1, 2022

Printed in the United States of America

ISBN 979-8-9866221-0-1 Trade Paperback

ISBN 979-8-9866221-1-8 eBook

# Dedication

T HE JOURNEY HERE WOULD not have been possible without the help of my beautiful, brown-eyed wife, who has been on this bumpy adventure with me for over twenty years. Thank you for being supportive and for a bright future ahead!

Several others have been impactful on this adventure. Purple Ninja Editorial had sage editorial advice. It was great to work with someone excited about science fiction! Appreciation to the team from Author Packages, and patience on development of the image of Tamir-Benob. There was a lot of back and forth with great imagination. A final appreciation for the map work of Thomas Shepherd and his authentic drawings. The maps add much more believability to the tale.

# The Genesis 6 Project

# Historical Perspective

"For which reason they removed their camp to Hebron; and when they had taken it, they slew all the inhabitants. There were till then left the race of giants, who had bodies so large, and countenances so entirely different from other men, that they were surprising to the sight, and terrible to the hearing. The bones of these men are still shown to this very day, unlike to any credible relations of other men."

Jewish Antiquities 5.23

Titus Flavius Josephus,
(37 AD–100 AD)
Jewish Scholar

# Cast of Characters

**Dr. Brian Simmons** – Archaeology professor

**Captain Julio Rodriguez** – Ranger Team Leader

**Captain Kathryn Ryan** – Military physician

**Frank Ironhorse Whitman** – Indian Affairs Agent

**General Cameron Briggs** – Leader of DEVCOM

**Giovanni De Luca** – Council of Five security team

**Gunther Muller** – Council of Five security chief

**Jim Blackhawk** – Indian Affairs law enforcement

**Klaus van Wilhelm** – Council of Five Vice Chair

**LTC Stephen Mullins** – Leader research lab

**Harold Stone** – Head of private security team

**Tamir-Benob** – Subject Alpha, captured by military

**The Chancellor** – Leader of the Council of Five

**Thomas Mighty Eagle** – Tribal medicine man

**Uri Goldberg** – Private security team member

# Prologue

**T**HE DESOLATE CAVE TUCKED away in the mountains had served as his home for several centuries following his forced migration. The elevation and year-round snow made it difficult for others to traverse on foot. A far cry from his youth in the plush valleys near the base of Mount Hermon. The few village tribesmen aware of his presence refrained from speaking about him from fear of his retribution.

On his last reconnaissance, he witnessed soldiers nearby, supported by large flying metal birds with fire weapons. The interlopers were becoming more frequent and beginning to intrude on his hunting grounds. The soldiers were unaware of his presence for now as he lurked in the afternoon shadows watching silently.

Earlier human inhabitants of his adopted home were more respectful of his presence, and even brought offerings to appease him. For a brief period, his kind communicated with humans, but not anymore. His people had a long history as mighty warriors, but that had changed. With the increasing arrogance of man, those who had the misfortune of encroaching on his abode were killed without mercy. As humans grew in number and power his kind had been forced to retreat, and their numbers dwindled. The Christian Templar Knights and other religious groups had made it a priority to eliminate his brothers. The last of his children died over five hundred years ago, something he planned to remedy.

In the barren lands he lived in today there was warring between foreign soldiers with firesticks and those trying to establish a religious caliphate.

Fighting over religious differences had always been man's downfall, especially if they understood how little difference it made to the Creator, he thought. Over the last thousand years, the various battles between human factions did little to change the scope of power. Many in this land still lived as simple tribesman, struggling to get through each day. Their main concern was to stay alive and feed their family. Although recently he killed a group of hunter-soldiers near his cave. They had been tracking him, which was concerning. How would they have been aware of his presence?

He had spent a great deal of time over the years hiding his tracks and remaining unseen. Any human had become an enemy. As the unnamed one reflected on his past, he sensed others approaching his hidden abode even now. This was a second intrusion in less than a week. The powder from their firesticks invaded his nose, and the slight scuffing of softly placed footsteps sounded loud to his ultra-sensitive ears. They were controlling their rate of breathing, a disciplined group. They were coming in stealth, trying to take him by surprise. Numerous scents suggested a team of nine, possibly ten men approaching. His spear and sword lay nearby.

If he acted quickly and took them by surprise, they would be no match for him. *Time to become the hunter.* His heartbeat quickened in anticipation.

The covert Army Special Forces squad leader was apprehensive as they approached the opening of the cave. The temperature was just below freezing, with a slight wind blowing. Their progress had been slowed by ice and pockets of snow. Thorny bushes partially blocked the cave entrance, but the soldiers were close enough to see inside the dimly lit opening. Several US troops had gone missing recently, and tracks led to here. Empty shell casings were scattered nearby suggesting a recent firefight. No other signs of the missing troops were evident. Intelligence reports from the locals and thermal imaging from overhead drones pointed to an unknown creature, big and humanoid in appearance waiting in the cave. A human this large should not exist and appeared more like a large bear. Although none of that added up. The squad leader kept his thoughts to himself, better not to spook the team.

Most of the men on the mission were seasoned fighters who had served on multiple covert missions. Each brought laser focus, the type of concentration one expected from those who experience danger frequently. They were equipped with M4A1 carbine assault rifles, but had orders to capture the beast in the cave with tranquilizers, an activity fraught with danger. A lone sniper was positioned as a failsafe with a standard Mk.11 Mod.0 sniper rifle. The team had worked several odd missions in the past, but this was the most secretive and was approved by those well above the Department of Defense chain of command. There was an eerie silence while the men waited with weapons trained and in offensive positions. Seconds seemed like hours as the team inched closer. The squad leader motioned for forward movement with his fingers.

Without warning, a large blur of a creature dressed in animal skins arose from the darkness of the cave entrance. The beast's eyes were piercing bright orange with menacing dark black pupils. Several soldiers thought they heard growls as it approached with medieval weapons in hand.

"Command, this is Bravo 2-1, we have eyes on target, and engaging now! The target is moving incredibly fast!" screamed the team leader in his communication device.

Military leaders listened anxiously from a hidden location several miles away as the squad approached the unknown target.

The advance of the creature was swift, and he closed the distance with the soldiers in seconds. The brute towered over them by several feet and outweighed the biggest soldier by almost a thousand pounds.

As the nearest man shot at the giant, the hulking creature used his spear to impale the unlucky soldier, killing him instantly.

"Take cover, try to slow him down!"

Bullets from the troops had little effect. The creature spoke in what sounded like a Hebrew dialect and advanced on the others. The nearest soldier was stabbed in the heart and thrown several feet. One of the soldiers shot his small handheld rocket launcher and hit their attacker in the shoulder, stunning him. Smoke rose from the wounded creature as he stooped on one knee. The squad leader yelled at his men with the brief opening for attack.

"Shoot him with the tranquilizers now! We have to end this before he recovers!"

All the men focused their attention on taking their opponent down, firing simultaneously with this one chance. They carried a specially developed aluminum dart system with high powered $CO_2$ delivery guns, strong enough to pierce the skin of a rhinoceros. As the cornered quarry started to black out from the many darts that had hit him and the drugs in his system, he threw his spear in a final protest at the nearest soldier scoring a solid hit. With an agonizing cry the beast fell over and passed out.

Slowly, the soldiers gathered around the unconscious giant with weapons raised, mindful that he may awake. The team worked quickly to secure him for evacuation. A transport helicopter had landed in the distance. A lift truck with a pallet made its way from the flying military bird to help in transport.

Numerous men worked together to load the giant on the pallet and ensure the creature was finally secured for transport. A C-130 Hercules with in-air refueling capabilities would then be used to cross the ocean and finally to a secret genetics research lab in the US.

On inspection, the cave that the creature emerged from went on for miles, and no signs of others like him were present. The smell inside the cave, which was littered with bones from previous kills and cannibalized humans, was overwhelming.

Also present were paintings showing battles and what appeared to be older script written on the wall. Weapons from conquered enemies and several parchments were found before a team demolished the cave entrance to prevent prying eyes from discovery. The soldiers on the extraction team sent their fallen comrades back home under a cover story, and then moved onto their next clandestine mission. The soldiers would never be told the purpose of the current capture of the creature and would be sworn to secrecy with nondisclosures and promised punishment if they talked about what they had witnessed.

The call was picked up after the first ring.

General Briggs answered in a gruff voice. "What news do you have for me Sanchez?"

"The extraction team subdued the target and is preparing him now for transport."

"Good. Were there any problems and how soon before departure?"

"The target was taken alive, but there were three casualties. We are sanitizing the area. I anticipate take off in less than fifteen minutes."

"Make sure the squad's debriefed appropriately when they write up their final reports."

"Understood, General." And with that the call ended abruptly.

In the United States, the Pentagon staff alerted the military facility in Montana with the news that their test subject would be arriving in the next twenty-four hours. Security went on high alert.

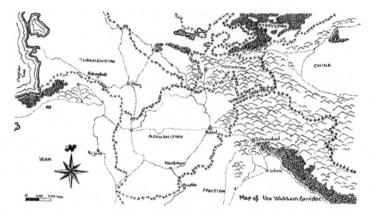

*Encounter with Subject Alpha*

# The Genesis 6 Project

# Chapter One

# Arrival of the Top Secret Cargo

**D**R. MULLINS WAS ALERTED as the flights quickly approached the military compound. The Boeing CH-47 Chinook transport helicopter was flanked by two other smaller unmarked black choppers. Timing was purposely planned for the middle of the night to avoid suspicion from the locals. A specialized private security team of former elite special forces soldiers provided support, and the compound included a maximum-security holding cell for high-value targets. The medical and security teams were waiting in the landing area as the choppers landed. Soldiers exited the Chinook as soon as it touched the ground, and Mullins stepped forward.

"I'm Lieutenant Colonel Mullins, base commander. We have been waiting for your arrival. My team will take the delivery from here."

After unloading the cargo, the soldiers reboarded without speaking, and the flying birds disappeared into the night as quickly as they had arrived.

Subject Alpha, named for the first of his kind, was taken swiftly to the containment cell. Their new state-of-the-art facility was housed in a basement-level building built on the outskirts of Billings, Montana, near the Crow Indian Reservation. The ruralness of the location was part of the reason for the far-out facility. Organizationally, the lab was part of DEVCOM, the research arm of the Army Futures Command.

Mullins had spent years training as a surgeon and soldier for an opportunity to lead this elite team of medical researchers. He could have left for the private sector, as several companies had approached him. But his calling was something big and impactful, and he needed a large organization to make that happen.

As their facility was designated as top secret, it rarely appeared on a briefing report, and then only for select levels of leadership. Their group was the flagship lab of the soldier development program and collaborated frequently with the Defense Department's DARPA group. The Pentagon was closely monitoring this project. Positive results could place them years ahead of any foreign adversary.

"Dr. Ryan let's get the subject secure and start testing right away. The general will want a briefing as soon as possible."

"We're on it, Dr. Mullins."

Subject Alpha had arrived unconscious, and the team intended to keep it that way. Senior military leaders were nervous about the risk of bringing such a dangerous entity into the US. If Montana officials ever got wind of this, there would be congressional hearings.

The lab had never employed such tight security before, and this would be a test for the security team at the facility. In the past, they had contained primates following genetic engineering with strength augmentation, but this was a much bigger challenge. The restrained being was many times stronger than any genetically enhanced primate. Mullins did not like using such extreme measures, but this was an incredibly dangerous situation, and the subject had already killed several highly trained soldiers.

The containment room also doubled as a surgical suite and makeshift lab. To maintain security, they were using multiple reinforced chains and hinged handcuffs on two oversized custom-made beds. For safety considerations they used two sets of reinforced handcuffs simultaneously. There was a constant flow of rapid IV sedation into the unconscious subject to ensure he never reached full consciousness. Vitals were monitored constantly to gauge alertness. They had sleeping gas ready to be deployed in seconds if needed. Although at some point they intended to try and communicate with the subject, which meant waking him up. Video cameras were set up in multiple locations in the room and fed to the security team.

For room integrity, the walls were built with concrete and reinforced steel that was several inches thick. Sliding doors were made of solid steel and included electrical locks. This setup would hold a charging elephant in place. As a fail-safe, electrical floor mats lined the entry-exit areas near the doors. A large electrical current with enough charge to slow the most powerful man down could be sent to anyone standing on the mats.

Stationed at each corner of the holding room were heavily armed special operation soldiers. They were the epitome of calm, cool, and lethal. A squad of six additional former and current elite soldiers were outside the containment room monitoring activity. On the facility grounds several more military and private security were available if needed. Although safeguards were in place, staff were understandably nervous.

As morning arrived, Mullins decided to gauge readiness with his team.

"How are things progressing," he said as he handed Dr. Ryan a cup of coffee.

"So far, so good. The subject is still sedated, and we will have preliminary results as early as tomorrow. The DNA sequencing will take longer, but the team is working overtime."

"Excellent, very good start. I know the team is anxious, but we'll do this in a way to ensure everyone's safety and that no harm comes to the subject."

Mullins thought to push the team harder, but held back, giving Ryan a chance to lead.

"There's still the concern about imprisoning the subject like this and making sure he's treated in a humane manner," Dr. Ryan cautioned.

"Understood, and you'll have a say in how we proceed with the captive. Need I remind you he killed three servicemen with only a spear and sword and is extremely dangerous? He likely exhibits extra human traits. The security is intended to protect our team more than anything. We must ensure there's no escape into the general public at all costs," Mullins stated matter-of-factly.

"Yes, but I'm still not going to allow him to be treated inhumanely," Dr. Ryan said with determination as they continued to walk and talk.

Dr. Kathryn Ryan was a career-military army captain who oversaw the genetics and biochemistry testing for the research lab. The Colorado native was an introvert, but the military had given her focus and confidence after medical school. Instead of a prestigious fellowship, she chose the military and a life of research. Her natural inquisitive nature led her to this point, but a goal of helping others drove her. Unfortunately, her long hours and constant travel contributed to her lack of a relationship, and at times a lonely life. In her little downtime, she was dedicated to fitness to match her mental prowess.

She sensed something ominous about the captive prisoner, and none of the research team wanted to be in the presence of the sleeping giant for any significant period of time. Although the creature was asleep, Ryan got the impression that he was watching and studying the team. As she walked away from

Mullins, Ryan thought to herself that something evil was present, and she had a foreboding feeling. *Were they opening a pandora's box?*

Security lead Harold Stone watched the interaction between the physicians with nervousness. The former Army Ranger led the protective services team assigned to the operation. Stone had spent over ten years in the military before retiring to a more lucrative contract security business. Private security companies performed a lot of the fighting and protection around the world, especially in high-risk areas. Stone tried to select missions that had purpose. But in many instances, he chose the most lucrative ones, which often put him in questionable moral situations. He was far away from the small Kansas town he grew up in.

Motion detectors were being installed to track the captive in the event the creature decided to make any sudden movements. Although detecting movement wouldn't stop the behemoth, security would at least have a heads up if there was an attempted escape. In Stone's assessment, something was still off, but he couldn't quite put his finger on it. There were many odd things he witnessed in his travels around the world, but any time an experimental subject had to be flown in by the military in the middle of the night to avoid civilian detection, danger was implied. His team had never dealt with a security threat like this, even in the most remote locations. The most lethal assassin didn't bring this level of preparation. At least with a bad actor there was some degree of psychosis that could be predicted. With this creature, they had little to base a risk assessment on and possibly no armament that could stop their prisoner. Not a promising thought.

Stone gave a nod of acknowledgement as a lab technician obtained a blood sample from the sleeping subject.

"Things are good on our end," Stone said, trying to reassure the lab members in the room, even as he felt something bad heading their way.

Two days had passed since Subject Alpha had arrived. Mullins was holding a staff briefing to review early results and discuss the dangers of waking the sleeping giant. His medical staff was gathered in a plush conference room of the facility. The room had the appearance of a corporate boardroom, except it was underground at a highly secure military facility. Senior members of Army Command were listening through a secure channel.

"Our preliminary findings suggest differences in this specimen's morphology and physiological makeup compared to modern human. His cross-sectional muscle fiber shows much greater area and density, meaning greater strength and endurance capacity. Amazingly, his telomere length in early DNA testing shows no shortening, which we know is a marker for longevity. Based on this information and the fact that the writings in the cave appear to be made over several hundred years ago by the same individual, we may be dealing with a species that is several hundred or a thousand years old," Dr. Mullins explained.

Most of those in the room were in disbelief and waited for him to continue.

"Not biologically possible," one of the lab techs mumbled to a colleague. He received a frown from Dr. Mullins in return.

"He was measured at a standing height just over eleven feet, weighing over twelve hundred pounds. His bone density scores were severalfold greater than a normal human, which allows him to support increased weight and ambulate normally. He appears to be an exception to the square-cube law. Some of his unique features include his elongated incisors and six fingers and toes on each extremity. A second row of teeth is present. The subject appears to have an enhanced healing factor and is probably immune to many diseases. We do not know yet his ability to verbally communicate, but we suspect the capability is present. His outward appearance is more like a large neanderthal, and his intelligence is probably very high if we accept the premise that he wrote the parchments in the cave and managed to stay hidden for all these years. Not only is this a new species of man but a hybrid of some type and not likely a product of genetic manipulation.

We recommend waking the subject under a very controlled, stepwise, secure manner. There's a plan to communicate with him, but we need to be mindful about our long-term anesthesia impact and adverse events. A translator is working on the written material found, and it is probably early Hebrew, but we'll let the experts decide," Mullins continued.

A question came from the back of the room.

"Dr. Mullins, you mentioned full testing of DNA samples. When will that work be complete?"

"We have adequate tissue samples. Some work has started here, and a sample will be sent by courier to the core lab in North Carolina for verification of results. It will take months or maybe years before there are any actionable results for our soldier program."

"When you wake the subject, are you sure we can keep him under control? Are risks mitigated, we can't have an escape. That would be unthinkable," General Briggs emphasized.

"That is our biggest concern. We are confident in our calculations, and we plan to bring the subject out slowly without completely awaking him to minimize risk. Anesthesia can be administered quickly if he awakes, and the security team is armed with tranquilizer darts, the same used with our initial capture. For added assurances, the containment room is reinforced and will hold him even if the first mitigation steps fail. So, you can feel confident about our ability to keep him contained. If by chance the subject escapes the lab area, there are over twenty Army Rangers and private security ready to engage him and prevent him from leaving the compound."

"I don't feel good about this, but it's satisfactory for now. How soon before the language translation, and when will you wake the thing up?" General Briggs pressed.

"The translation should be ready in the next twelve hours, and shortly after that he will be awakened. But we're confirming with the professor."

After a long pause and an icy stare, the general spoke again. "Stone, do you agree with the colonel's assessment?"

"I do. We are prepared."

"Ok, let's move forward and make initial contact before his transport. There's a location for long-term confinement that I'll share later." The general took a pause, ended the meeting, and closed out the video conference.

Mullins could sense the medical team was scared and unsettled by the general's comments.

"Ok folks let's keep working. You heard the general. Let's finish our preliminary testing and focus on our mission. Dr. Ryan will be running point. The security team will be pressure testing different scenarios again. In a couple days this will be over."

As the group dissipated, Dr. Ryan approached Dr. Mullins. "Could I speak to you for a moment when the others leave?"

"Sure, what's on your mind?"

"Are you positive it's smart to wake Subject Alpha? This is a dangerous situation. We probably have the most destructive creature on the planet locked in that room, and we have no idea how he will respond or our ability to contain him. He's probably back at full strength by now," Ryan reminded him.

"I understand your trepidation. But this is an opportunity of great scientific and military importance. This is only the beginning, and the possibilities are endless. We'll be extremely cautious and take things slowly. You'll be deciding how fast we progress in our wake-up protocol. Ok?"

"I'm not convinced about our safety, but it seems there's no stopping things, even if I went to General Briggs."

"Yes, General Briggs is pushing for this step. We would prefer you be involved." Although not satisfied, Ryan decided to go along with Mullins and gauge the angle he was playing.

Tamir-Benob was aware of those around him, but he still lingered between unconsciousness and awake. The chatter of the human voices could be heard by his sleeping senses. Something kept his mind foggy and from waking completely. He knew his body would adapt and restraints would be meaningless. The bed and room that contained him was unknown. The last thing he remembered was the fight with the men in the cave. They shot him with their firesticks and other strange weapons. Those men were smarter than the tribesman he delt with over the years. They dressed differently and were more organized. It had been some time since he fought men such as these, perhaps as far back as the Christian Knights or even the Roman soldiers. No matter, he would be victorious. As he fell back asleep his body continued to heal at a rapid pace.

# Chapter Two

# Nearby at the Crow Reservation

FRANK IRONHORSE WHITMAN SAT in his Dodge Durango after finishing his early morning patrol. His team was responsible for numerous law enforcement activities across several American Indian reservations. As Assistant Special Agent in Charge of Indian Affairs, he was a senior official for District 5 overlapping several midwestern states. Hard work and lots of sleepless nights had led to his current position. He sipped on a bottle of chilled water and reflected on his past. Watching the elderly man walk with the boy across the street reminded him of a distant memory with his grandfather. Grandfather helped raise him after his mother had passed as a youth.

"Ironhorse, one day you will use the learnings of our people to guide and protect you. Respect the wisdom of the forest and listen to the wood spirits," Grandfather had reminded him.

"I hear nor see anything. How can I listen when the spirits do not speak?"

"Be patient young one, they speak. Trust your senses. You must practice and hone your skills. Now close your eyes and feel the wind against your cheek and in your hair. Focus on your breathing and take in the scent of the damp earth and the smell of the pine tree. Can you hear the bird singing softly? Open your ears and listen to the sounds of the branches rustling and the stream flowing. Can you hear the tiny patter of feet nearby?"

"Yes, Grandfather, I hear a slow stepping patter."

"Good, Ironhorse. Now turn slowly to your left without a sound, open your eyes, and tell me what you see."

As he opened his eyes, he saw a small rabbit chewing green grass nearby. The white rabbit did not move but eyed him with blue eyes as a friend in the forest. Ironhorse was surprised at his ability to observe once he concentrated.

"If you listen closely to the sounds, the forest will provide and protect you. Remember that" his grandfather had said.

As he grew older, Ironhorse better understood the teachings of his grandfather. Carefully using his senses to take in his surroundings had saved him more than once before.

He missed his grandfather and remembered being brash and bold while trying to overly balance his early tribal learnings with too much modern society. He started down the path of deviant behavior. Although joining the military right after high school was the change, he needed to avoid the remorse and sadness he had felt from the loss of family, it had been difficult for the rest of his family to accept his far away military service.

Whitman was a natural fit for the US Army Rangers and was stationed with the Seventy-Fifth Regiment at Fort Benning, Georgia. During his service, he completed secret tours in the Middle East. There was more than enough death and destruction with all the unexplained happenings—strange noises in the night, unknown humanoid looking tracks in the sand, legends of nocturnal spirits, and a few sightings of large creatures on mountain patrols that shouldn't exist. The vanishing man wearing a white hoodie he tracked through the mountains on patrol was particularly troubling, there one minute, looking at him with a dark evil scowl and black eyes, and then gone a moment later with no explanation. It was certainly something he did not write up in a report.

The training of his youth had kept him sane during that time, or at least safe, as he was convinced there were many unexplained things in the world.

Unfortunately, he still had the occasional bad dream, but most of the residual PTSD was from the needless death he had witnessed.

He had been glad to get back to the states.

Joining the Department of Indian Affairs, or IA as many called it, after his military service was an honor. His tribe needed community service as there was an inadequate police department. His motto was that everyone should feel safe in their own community. Years of working long hours and taking night courses had finally paid off. His responsibility now included managing several departments, the highest profile a small special response group that was comparable to a SWAT team in big cities.

He checked the time and estimated his drive time to make the meeting with the Crow Tribe Executive Branch leadership team. Their monthly meetings could go on for a while, and in many cases tribal leaders were more concerned with exerting their influence than completing their meeting agenda.

His mind wondered a bit again. It would be nice to spend time with his daughter and enjoy a single father-daughter lunch later. That would be the highlight of his day, but wow did she keep him busy. His days as an overly protective father were winding down and he wasn't looking forward to her starting to date the local boys.

⟫⟫ ⟪⟪

After a long morning at the Native Council American Indians meeting, Agent hitman was finishing up lunch at his favorite sandwich shop with his daughter when he received a troubling call from his sergeant, Jim Blackhawk.

"Frank, I need to update you on a call that just came in, and it's troubling."

"Give it to me, Jim," Whitman said, as he motioned to his daughter that he would be busy for a minute or two.

"Sally Running Horse, who lives southwest of Indian Arrow, called. She was upset about another late-night helicopter flyover. This was worse than the last flyby. Seems there were at least three choppers. Woke her after 2:00 a.m. Animals on the farm were startled and several ran away. One of the choppers was larger than the others. Her description sounded military in appearance, and they were moving fast. She only saw them briefly. No one else in her family observed them. I told her we would investigate further." Jim paused for a minute and then continued "Think it's another covert military training exercise? Sounds similar to last time, but we never received a straight answer from our sources on that one."

Whitman was perplexed. "Thanks, Jim. Sounds military. Go ahead and check it out. It is strange that several helicopters would be flying in so late. Doesn't sound like a training exercise."

*Why would a remote region near the Crow reservation be of interest to the military?* Thought Whitman.

"This is a bad pattern. My gut leans toward a mission-oriented flyby or transport of something important, and very covert. See if any others on the reservation observed anything and reach out to our military liaison again. Keep me posted if you hear anything on this," Whitman said.

⤜⤜⤜ ⤛⤛⤛

Later that evening Stone finalized the security protocol with his team. Subject Alpha was secure, restraints and anesthesia levels were being checked every fifteen minutes by his men. He decided to take a quick smoke break outside the facility; it was one of his few vices.

The sky was clear and crisp, such a peaceful evening. Odd, someone else was outside, although he couldn't see or hear who it was.

Must be someone from the medical team taking a breather, thought Stone. He couldn't make out their conversation, as they had their back to him, and it looked like they were dialing on a cell phone. Given the day ahead and having already completed the necessary background checks on the lab staff, he decided not to bother them or worry about security. Stone wanted to enjoy his smoke while the unknown soldier continued their conversation on the other side of the courtyard.

"Yes, it's me," the unknown soldier spoke softly into their phone, using the darkness to hide their identity from a remote Stone.

A slow, measured voice with a slight European accent answered, "Status update?"

"Subject Alpha is still under anesthesia, and DNA samples have been obtained for our use as planned. There are no suspicions from the others of what we are doing."

"Are there enough samples for amplification and gene editing for our planned projects?"

"Yes, plenty with our PCR technology, and contact has been made with the courier for the transport to Europe."

"Excellent. And feasibility of subject acquisition and transport? Having the subject available to question on its history would be ideal."

"The best chance of capture is after the hybrid's escape. I will proceed as planned and reduce anesthesia discreetly. Resistance from base security at that point will be lowest, although still a challenge. An escape will allow the distraction needed for courier departure."

"Good if we can capture the subject during his rampage, but if not, at a minimum we will have samples for the next phase of our plan. We will await your signal for timing and coordinates for our extraction team. They are nearby and can initiate on a moment's notice. The team leader is aware you will be traveling with them on departure to our location to supervise the next steps. Transport will be via helicopter when the time is appropriate. But don't forget our expectations are high and future plans are predicated on the success of this mission. This operation cannot fail, and you know what failure means," emphasized the caller.

"Yes, there will be no failure. I will do my part to make sure the subject escapes and give the extraction team information they need."

"We will talk soon then." The caller abruptly hung up.

There was a little fear for the American agent, but there was more elation about the chance of success. Years of planning had finally produced an opportunity such as this. Tireless study of the religious texts and now success was in sight. Time to go back inside to avoid suspicion from the other team members for being absent. The charade would only last a little longer. He took a deep breath, regained his composure, and headed back into the facility.

⠿⠿ ⠿⠿

Whitman was troubled by the previous day's report of helicopters flying over the Crow reservation. Their investigation turned up little as expected, and their military liaisons were no help. Reservation land was protected federal land, and someone with top secret clearance was encroaching. Jim Blackhawk had driven out to the area and found little signs of activity. Something was coming, the feeling inside him was overwhelming. He decided to stop by the office of his friend Thomas Mighty Eagle. Thomas had been mentored by Whitman's grandfather and served as spiritual guide for the tribe. They had been childhood friends.

"How are things going Ironhorse?" the stoic medicine man asked and greeted him with a handshake and pat to the shoulder.

"I am well my friend, but have been bothered by recent dreams, and this awful feeling of a coming evil. I awake at night with sweats and always end up being chased by a large red-haired, faceless warrior."

"Sit, and let's discuss the signs," Mighty Eagle said, handing him a cup of strong coffee. There was just enough time to catch up before training with his team.

⟶⟫⟫ ⟪⟪⟵

Whitman returned home late from a long day of training in Wyoming. Tomorrow he would be with his group's version of the special operations police unit, similar to a SWAT unit. The small unit was specialty trained in tactics and hostage negotiation and included a sniper. They regularly trained to keep their skills honed, including a recent FBI counter-terrorism course. He felt confident in their ability to take on most challenges. After saying goodnight to his daughter, he headed to bed for a restful night's sleep and an early rise.

He took a few minutes to catch up on some reading, but his thoughts went back to his conversation with Thomas Mighty Eagle. Whitman's friend had cautioned him that he was being given warning of a danger approaching the tribe. Whitman had mixed feelings on the spirit world, but his family and friends felt he should embrace this side of his heritage. What to make of a large, red-haired warrior was a puzzling piece indeed. Mighty Eagle had reminded him of his tribe's long-ago history with this ancient adversary. His grandfather would be able to interpret this if he had still been alive, but for now he would have to ponder it another day. There were real bad guys he needed to focus on now, and none of them were large red-haired warriors who carried spears.

Whitman finished the training exercise with his special operations team the next morning. He enjoyed live action training the best because it provided an opportunity to practice tactical scenarios and weapons training. His group used military-grade weapons when they were available, and although rarely needed, they gave the team a degree of comfort when challenged by the most violent criminal element. Unfortunately, they'd had to deal with drug smugglers and hostage situations just in the past year. His go-to weapon was a Glock 19 9 mm, but he also felt comfortable with a Colt M4 Carbine and a .308 Winchester when he needed more firepower. The team consisted of American Indians who were proficient in modern police weapons as well as the more traditional tribal weapons for striking and piercing in nonlethal situations.

# Chapter Three
# Awakening the Beast

**A**S THE MEDICAL TEAM began to reduce Subject Alpha's sedation, everyone in the makeshift operating room grew anxious. He would be awakened slowly in a controlled manner. Communication with the captive would be their top priority, but anesthesia could be used quickly if the situation grew dangerous. Uri, a former soldier in the Israeli Defense Force, now served on the private security team. He would be useful if the subject spoke in Hebrew as was reported by the extraction team.

Dr. Mullins watched as Dr. Ryan and the team cautiously awakened Subject Alpha. His eyelids fluttered briefly. The moment was at hand. His fingers moved slightly, heart rate and respiration increased. They were making history.

Tamir-Benob was finally able to hear them speak. He did not understand their language yet, but his preternatural cognitive ability allowed him to learn languages quickly. It was difficult to open his eyes, but the anesthesia was becoming less effective. His arms felt heavy like tree trunks, but that would soon pass. Feigning sleepiness would test him, but he needed to be cautious before he acted. Patience was difficult for him as he only understood strength and decisiveness.

"He is waking!" yelled one of the anxious team members. The room was on edge.

Subject Alpha slowly opened his eyes. Tamir-Benob felt groggy and couldn't raise up. He studied the room through blurry sight, counting those present, observing the soldiers. The fear in the room could be smelled. His arms and feet were held in place, and he couldn't move them. The room was quiet with anticipation.

Dr. Mullins and his team tried unsuccessfully to communicate with Subject Alpha. Multiple languages were used without a breakthrough.

"Can you hear us? Can you see us? What is your name? He is not responding. Uri, can you speak to him in Hebrew?"

Uri, one of the private security soldiers, stepped closer. He held his assault rifle close. Although a big man at over six feet tall, he felt exceedingly small compared to the creature on the bed. Uri spoke in Hebrew.

"I asked him if he understood, and if he had a name," a cautious Uri explained.

Tamir-Benob understood the question and grimaced in response. The language of those long ago who killed his father and uncle. The language of a race who should be servants of his kind. He thought of the men from the past who forced him to leave his homeland of Philistia and spend a miserable millennium in caves. If not for them, his kind would have ruled the world. Anger rose deep inside him, but he controlled the urge to snap the young soldier's neck. Staying silent was his way of forcing the move of his captors.

"Something upset him, Uri. Can you explain we mean no harm but want to learn more about his history?" Mullins directed him.

Uri repeated his questions in Hebrew. All eyes were on the prisoner, waiting any response.

After a short pause he addressed them in Hebrew, looking directly at Uri with a malevolent gaze.

Uri translated with a look of horror, "I will be your destruction, as you should have stayed away. Your weapons cannot protect you. Free me now and I will let some of you live."

The team looked at each other in shock. Before anyone could speak Subject Alpha snapped one of the handcuffs and grabbed Uri and his two hundred pounds by the neck effortlessly. The sheer speed of the attack left the soldier off guard, and he tried to butt the giant in the face with his M4A1 service rifle. Two other soldiers jumped in to help restrain him. Uri screamed as his wrist was crushed in the vicelike grip of the giant's hand.

Dr. Ryan hurried over to administer more sedation into the IV.

"Call the others to help restrain the subject. We have a minute before the sedation kicks in," a shaken Dr. Ryan screamed.

An evil stare, devoid of emotion like no one had ever seen, was plastered across the creature's face.

Security rushed into the room to help restrain the subject. The red-haired giant let out a primordial roar and threw two soldiers back across the room effortlessly. He attempted to stand up, but the weight of the frantic soldiers and additional sedation kept him from rising. Slowly the anesthesia worked, and Subject Alpha closed his eyes and became motionless like a statue. Restraints were quickly fastened in place. Stone escorted an injured Uri out of the room to provide first aid and called a replacement for him.

Mullins tried to take control of a difficult situation. "How is everyone holding up?"

He was met by shaky gazes and brief nods, so he gave orders for each of them, more to keep them busy than anything else. This was a critical moment.

"Stone, when Uri has a moment to recover ask if he understood anything else the subject said. We have translation of some of the cave material arriving later today. That should give us a little more insight. I will speak to General Briggs about expediting the move of the subject to a more secure location. We can continue to work on genetic analysis."

Mullins continued to assess the shaken team and tried to provide more encouragement. "This was a little unnerving, but we know what we're dealing with now. Let's keep his escape effort as a one-time event."

As the research team went about their work and the excitement died down Dr. Ryan confronted Dr. Mullins.

"I would like to speak with you in private."

"Sure, lets step to the side office," he replied as he motioned down the hallway.

Dr. Ryan could barely contain her anger long enough for Dr. Mullins to close the door. "At this point we need to terminate our work here and move the subject to a more secure location. This is way too dangerous. Next time someone will die. We can barely contain that thing!"

"I hear what you're saying, Dr. Ryan, but this is the last opportunity we have with the subject before he's taken away. A once in a lifetime chance. Think of what we can learn, not only for soldier benefit but for medicine and history. As a scientist doesn't that intrigue you?"

"That doesn't lower the risk to the team, Dr. Mullins. I protest this course of action and will go to Briggs if I have to. This simply isn't safe."

"Our security team is here to mitigate the risk. The parchment translations will provide more insight. You can take this to Briggs. I won't order you to participate. It'll be your choice, but we're moving forward with or without you," Mullins said adamantly.

"I'm going on record as having warned you this is a mistake."

"You're more than welcome to do that, Captain Ryan, and I'll warn you that's likely not a great career choice. We all knew there would be risks. Now we have work to get back to." With that Mullins turned and left the room.

⟫⟩ ⟨⟪

Dr. Mullins stepped into the conference room still heated from his exchange with Dr. Ryan, but he needed to put it out of his mind. General Briggs was waiting for his update.

"General, one more effort is needed to communicate with the subject. This is our best chance to learn more about his background and origins, especially since he is disoriented. The more we know about him the further we'll be able to take our program. He's disoriented and over time will become more guarded. Security has been enhanced, and we know what we're dealing with now. In a few hours we'll be able to share the translation from the cave with you before moving ahead."

"One last shot Mullins. Don't screw it up. Set up the camera in the lab so we can have a direct feed. If anything at all is out of line, we pull the plug. Let's hear the translation and determine if it's biblically related as you suggest. We need more before sharing with leadership. I honestly still can't believe this creature is as old as you suggest. None of this will change my mind about keeping him stateside; he's being sent to Camp Delta at Guantanamo. We have maximum security detention areas there that can house the subject securely. Gitmo will have a makeshift medical facility set up according to your specifications, and you will need to fly down to supervise the research on-site."

"Understood, sir. We will proceed then. Our briefing on the translation will be in approximately two hours. The archaeological specialist will be on the call to answer questions."

"In addition to my staff, a few others from the National Security Agency will be listening in." General Briggs ended the call gruffly and hung up before Mullins could respond.

A few hours later Mullins assembled his team in the basement for the call with the army archaeological experts. The general and his staff were listening on the secure feed.

"Dr. Simmons, you can begin the briefing," Mullins ordered.

"Thank you, Colonel. We just finished our preliminary analysis a few minutes ago. A variety of documents and cave writings are still under review. Writing on parchment and vellum from animal skins was taken from the cave. Radiocarbon dating found the oldest writings to be from around the year 1000 BC, and the most recent was approximately five hundred years ago. The handwriting on the parchments looks identical throughout, meaning the same person probably wrote on the parchment over the approximate three-thousand-year period."

"Hold on, Doctor. You're saying this creature is over three thousand years old? That can't be true!" an exasperated General Briggs stated.

"General, the evidence suggests that, but we need to recheck to verify."

"Go on, but I'm skeptical." The general turned and whispered something to one of his staff.

"The language of the writings was an older Hebrew script, commonly used during the time of King David and Solomon. Based on our analysis, Subject Alpha appears to have moved across the Middle East region in a nomadic pattern, starting around the Israel-Palestine area.

Cave portraits depicted battles with large middle eastern armies, and the parchments discussed battles in exotic lands that are now part of modern-day Iraq, Iran, and others. Over the years he made his way to his current home. Some of the weapons and remnant clothing in the cave suggest he used it as a home base for the last several hundred years. This was an exceedingly difficult location to travel by foot, given its remoteness and high elevation. Only an exceptionally strong individual could survive in this area for any length of time. It would have provided an ideal location to stay hidden. He certainly would have been predatory given the amount of human remains found, most likely from the unwary tribesman or even actively hunting soldiers and villagers."

"Were there any weapons found in the cave?" General Briggs asked.

"Yes. There were US military weapons found. Several broken assault rifles and a pile of spent shells. We can assume that some of the missing troops were killed by Subject Alpha. None of their bodies were in the cave, although there were several human bones in the cave," Dr. Simmons replied. "Interestingly, several other weapons found predating the modern age were probably used by Subject Alpha. There were a few spears, swords, and shields. Some dated as far back as the Roman Empire, but most were handmade from the last few hundred years. One spear was over ten feet long and weighed over seventy-five pounds. The strength to wield that is much greater than a normal man would have been able to do."

"The beast's weapons were still viable then?" asked the General.

"Yes, they were made with remarkably good craftsmanship."

"Was there anything in the cave that suggested intelligence or clues to background?" asked Dr. Ryan.

"The soldiers did not find anything significant outside of the parchments. No personal belongings beyond weapons or clothing were there. They did find a small firepit in the back, so he may have used it to cook from time to time. The subject lived like a savage, albeit intelligent enough to write and to conceal himself for this long."

Dr. Simmons continued rapidly through his briefing.

"Let's review the translation of the self-history parchment," he said, as an image of the writings appeared on the screen.

*After the great waters receded in the lands of the Philistines, the sons of man multiplied. Our forefathers, the spirit sons, of YHVH, again walked amongst men and begat our elders, including my father Ishbi-Benob and his brother Goliath from*

*Gittite. For a short time these fallen were worshiped in temple, but brought the wrath of the Creator and his spirit soldiers. Over time Goliath and Ishbi-Benob grew to be mighty warriors of renown who felled strong armies with their superior skills and were feared throughout the land. My kind grew in number, and we begat children.*

*Near my land, the mighty King Saul challenged our people to free his tribes, although the chosen King feared us. Several of his holy men were killed by my kind. My kinsman Goliath led the Philistine army in battle but was killed by the sheepherding boy who went on to be king. With vengeance, Ishbi-Benob the Great, fought and injured the Hebrew warrior king who was an older warrior then. But my father was deceitfully killed by David's servant Abishai. I fought and killed many of the Hebrew warriors after that but was forced to leave my homeland. My people scattered to escape the wrath of YHVH's earthly king, going to all areas, including across the seas. I was the strongest of my kind, and my travel was far and battles many . . .*

"These writings suggest fallen angels from the Genesis 6 story of the Christian Bible were Subject Alpha's forefathers. The writer of the parchment goes on to say he is the nephew of Goliath, the giant from Gath who supposedly was killed by the future Israeli King David. I would say—"

"That is ludicrous, Simmons. You're telling us that Subject Alpha is some descendent of a biblical giant and fallen angels? This is a fairy tale. Surely you have more?" an agitated General Briggs pressed.

"I will point out that we are translating an old parchment found in the cave, and we can't be sure that Subject Alpha penned this, but it seems logical that he or someone close to him did. Remember, with many stories in mythology or ancient texts, there is usually a kernel of truth or some actual event that forms the basis of these stories. There are credible pieces of evidence, including giant human bones found in Britain, China, and even on American Indian reservations in the US. In some cases, entire skeletons were found, and remains ranged from eight to eleven feet tall. With our own eyes we are seeing a large humanoid male, larger than any man ever reported, with superhuman strength and resistance to many manmade weapons."

"I'm not convinced, and doubt the White House will be either, but go on."

Mullins and the team set impatiently listening to the archaeology professor. These were fantastic claims, but they could not explain what they were witnessing. There had to be a medical explanation for Subject Alpha.

Dr. Simmons continued, "Other parts of the parchment that mention kings and battles according to biblical history and nonbiblical sources occurred over thousands of years. This information is unlike any uncovered before and rival details found in the Dead Sea Scrolls. We have positively identified artifacts in the cave dating back to the Safavid Empire rulers around the year 1500 AD, and they are believed to be part of early Iranian history.. There were other types of small skirmishes mentioned, even one which references the Durrani Empire from around the early 1800s."

General Briggs interrupted. "Enough with the history lesson. This is far-fetched at best. How would Subject Alpha have remained undetected all these years?"

"General, from our understanding of the topography the nearest villages are more than thirty miles away, and the cave where he was found is over eleven thousand feet elevation, which stays cold and snowy. That's a very rough terrain, and very few people venture into that remote area. There's little history of military forces being involved in this part of the country. Heavy foliage and dense trees are everywhere, so unless he were out in the open, and given the clouds around the mountains, it would be difficult to spot him even from the air with a drone or plane.

I suspect if tribesman or hunters ventured out in that area and came across Subject Alpha, they met their demise. The few reports received by military sources from the locals were that they were scared to go near the caves, as there was a legend of a red-headed giant that ate little children. The villages nearby are still very remote, and traditional, without electricity. We believe the local militias even stayed clear of the region. This is a place where it would be very dangerous to be lost," Simmons explained.

"If this place was so inhospitable, how did Subject Alpha survive these harsh conditions?"

"He was dressed in animal skins at the time of his capture, and more were found in the cave. The firepit may have been used for heat when temperatures were extremely cold as well as for cooking. Based on reports from Dr. Mullins, Subject Alpha has a higher metabolism, better ability to regulate body heat, and in essence a built-in thermostat to handle wider variations in environmental conditions."

"That would be one heck of an advantage for the modern-day soldier," Briggs conceded.

"Indeed, but it will take years to figure out his biology," chimed in Dr. Ryan.

"General, I would like to address one more topic, which is rather concerning," said Dr. Simmons.

"Go on."

"The last translation relates to Subject Alpha's travels and plans. The translation is as follows." Dr. Simmons clicked a new slide onto the screen for the group to read.

*My brothers and I left our homeland of Philistia. We traveled through Persia and observed many wonders. Some kindred went to other lands, away*

43

*from the armies of YHVH. We conquered many men and their armies. Men feared us wherever we traveled. The Nephilim feasted on blood and ravished their women, creating offspring. Over time we were hunted by others, including the Christian Templar Knights, but traveled to faraway lands and the great caves. Men eventually built cities near our villages. We used their superstitions to enslave the tribes and killed many of their people. But man grew strong and built weapons. Over the ages most of our kind were killed, and few of our own children remained.*

*I was visited by other fallen sons of YHVH, who were powerful spirit men. Their power and might were like the gods of old. Their presence overwhelmed my senses. They cautioned for patience, and that soon there would be an awakening, and that others of their kind would return to fight the Hebrew God and his sons. They light of the star of the morning son would reemerge and lead us into battle. They told me of brothers who lived across the waters in the land of the mighty eagles, and who fought with the native men who communed with the great forest spirits. Our numbers are now small; but I remain committed to bringing our kind together and avenging the death of Ishbi-Benob through blood, so swears Tamir-Benob the Mighty.*

There was a lengthy silence as the group took it all in.

General Briggs was the first to speak. "Interesting, Dr. Simmons. Not sure how believable all this is. It's hard to consider giants and holy angel wars, but we do have an exceptional specimen that gives us a step ahead for our soldier enhancement program. We will learn from this one way or another. I do appreciate your work and opinions on this."

"Why don't we let Dr. Simmons go and continue with the briefing with the rest of the team," suggested Mullins.

As Dr. Simmons disconnected from the call, General Briggs continued, "Transport for Subject Alpha to Gitmo will arrive tomorrow. Dr. Mullins will be accompanying Subject Alpha on the trip with a team of his choice. We need to try to speak with the subject one last time if we can maintain security. Perhaps he will respond differently if we confront him with his history and how the world has changed."

"General, I must object to this course of action. We will not be able to control Subject Alpha. This is a big mistake!" an angry Dr. Ryan exclaimed.

"Captain Ryan, I understand your grave concern, but we're going to make one more effort, and I trust in the US military on this one," General Briggs said dismissively. "Stone, do you think we can provide adequate security in this situation?"

"We'll be more prepared this time," Stone assured the group. "He caught us off guard, but it's not going to happen again. We'll manage the situation going forward. Uri will also be able to translate for us even with his injuries."

"Very good. Let's prepare for another attempt later today, and pickup tomorrow," the general ordered.

➤➤➤ ⬅⬅⬅

Tamir-Benob caught the last part of the soldier's muffled discussion. He was becoming more aware of his surroundings as the effects of the sleeping agent began to wear off. His arms were less fatigued, and his body rested. The restraints on him were weak and easy to break. If he was patient, he would catch them by surprise. These were warriors, but they were shortsighted and relied on their strange science. His experiences over the last several years showed him how man had become reliant on technology. Later in the evening they would be more complacent, and it would be a good time to make his escape. Although this was a foreign land, he wondered if any of his brothers were still around. It had been ages since another of his kind had been seen.

# Chapter Four

# Commandos Arrive from Europe

**T**HE FOREIGN MEMBER STRIKE **team had made its** way to America, traveling separately on different commercial airlines. Each man traveled independently, as their mission was being kept confidential. Additional secrecy was maintained by using back roads to the rendezvous point. Contracted illicit arms dealers had arranged for weapons and heavy transport for their mission once the team arrived on American soil.

"Excellent. We will activate our men. They're close by and will move quickly. Be ready for our call."

Although they did not work for a government agency, the team was former military, and all were disciples of their new cause. Gunther, a massive muscular man and former German Kommando Spezialkräfte, was team leader. He was a battle-hardened veteran, with experience leading covert teams on most continents. He was a private man, with no immediate family, a perfect fit for a life as a career soldier. His one hobby was the collection and consumption of vintage spirits. The council had provided him with a lifetime supply for his work. The rest of his handpicked team were highly skilled soldiers and guns for hire, mostly from countries that were part of the Council of Five. The team had trained together for several months waiting for an opportunity such as this. They had reconvened and were waiting near the Montana military compound in a remote wooded area.

"Giovanni, are the men ready to go?" Gunther asked.

"They await our orders and have been briefed on our mission and its importance. Each understand the seriousness of our target. The extraction team will arrive this evening, and the ship to transport the package across the ocean is secured in port with our men in place."

"Good, I will speak to command later to receive our final orders. The US military will wake the subject later today, and as expected, they had a tough time controlling him during the first encounter. We should know something soon from our source, but we need to be ready to go at a moment's notice. Make sure the men bring extra armaments."

"Very good, Gunther. We have practiced much for this moment and will be ready," Giovanni replied.

⤜⤜⤜ ⤛⤛⤛

At the US military compound, Dr. Mullins was   preparing to wake Subject Alpha with a reluctant Dr. Ryan by his side. Security had been doubled since the last encounter with the subject, and the staff had been provided with tranquilizer guns. General Briggs and others were monitoring via video conference feed. Anesthesia to the subject had been reduced steadily over the last thirty minutes. The room was tense, only the slow continuous beat of the EKG attached to Subject Alpha could be heard.

"We are tracking an increase in heart rate, and there is eyelid movement. Alpha is waking now," said a nervous lab tech.

Tamir-Benob frowned slightly, and his animal like incisors hung down as he opened his eyes. He could see the fear in their eyes and their false confidence from the firesticks pointed at him. Shackles held him in place. Other unknowns were in the room, including attachments to his skin and something sharp piercing and running fluids into his arms. He was housed as a caged animal. Remaining quiet put them on edge but allowed him to study his captors. There were also females in the room, as to what role they played in this he did not understand.

Dr. Ryan studied their captive's orange eyes, which burned with fire and hate. His massive, chiseled face and his long, red hair reminded her of a Viking god. Certainly, no man or creature could contest the supremacy of this one in the wild. The giant

49

was baiting them, waiting on their response, like a cat with a mouse. More intelligence and cunning were there than others realized.

The question now was who would break first.

"Uri, ask the questions we discussed," snapped Dr. Mullins.

Tamir-Benob feigned indifference, but noted the one in charge—not as powerful looking as the others but led with an air of authority. They did not pick their leaders based on physical strength, something he found strange.

Uri spoke to the subject in Hebrew. "Tamir-Benob, do you understand? We mean you no harm. You are in an American army facility. Can you speak?"

Tamir-Benob showed no emotion as he stared at the soldier who spoke to him from several feet away. This was the young soldier he grabbed earlier. Material covered his wrist where he grabbed the youth. They awaited his response anxiously, although the women gave him a look of defiance. He smirked at them, with only evil intentions, realizing they had translated his self-parchment scroll.

Mullins directed Uri again. "Uri, he understands and is mocking us. Tell him the rest."

"You are a prisoner of the US military for crimes against our soldiers and humanity. You are going to be transported to another facility, by force if needed. We expect answers to our questions," Uri said to the giant.

Tamir-Benob laughed with a deep roar and answered in Hebrew. "Do you really think you can hold me? I have fought the mighty armies of Alexander and destroyed warriors from the Mongol empire. Thousands of men have felt my boot and died in battle. Great kings have feared my wrath. Why would you fare any better? My father was Ishbi-Benob, the son of a powerful fallen. My people were men of renown. You mean nothing to me. I will rip your head off your body and drink your warm blood. I will do with your women as a I please. Villages of your people will fall and worship me as in times past. Your time is short, now let me go." Raw strength flowed from the beast as he spoke.

An unnerved Uri translated the message to the team.

As the group looked at each other with fear, Mullins pushed back. "Uri, tell him we have questions for him to answer, and his threats mean nothing to us. Ask him to prove what he is saying and demand to know where he is from."

Stone sensed a change in posture from Subject Alpha, a preparation for action. The creature tensed, as in attack mode. The hairs on the back of Stone's neck rose as a dangerous omen. He moved closer and gripped his tranquilizer gun harder.

Tamir-Benob watched Stone move closer and slowly pointed a long bony finger at the security expert, assessing how far to test his jailers.

"You will be the first to die, soldier," Tamir-Benob warned. "Do you think you can keep me asleep sleep with your poison? You have taken my parchment of self-history. Where is the thief? You want to know my origins? I am from the great land of Philistia, near Hermon, the home of the Rapha and the great Og!"

As Uri translated Mullins yelled, trying to regain control. "Tell him we know where Philistia is located. Ask him if he is related to Goliath and if he battled the Hebrew King David."

Tamir-Benob looked with contempt at Mullins. "What do you think, leader of man? Your weapons will not harm me, and I am your elder. Many, many years older and wiser. Why would I tell you children, my ancient history? Are you worthy? Especially those who speak the language of my enemy, the dog called David."

Once again Mullins directed Uri. "Tell him we thought he was a great warrior and that he would tell us his exploits, if they are true. Tell him to answer our questions."

"Dr. Mullins stop this! You're only antagonizing him more. This is dangerous," pleaded Dr. Ryan.

Tamir-Benob sat further up in the bed and strained against his shackles which strained outward like they might break. He glared at Dr. Mullins, with the others in the room watched speechlessly.

He voice pierced like thunder. "I am beginning to learn your language. You should listen to the woman. You hold me prisoner and goad me about being a warrior? Only cowards restrain their enemies like this. Release me and I will show you a real battle. One day soon, my brothers will bring war and death to your kind. Your army and the Hebrew God will be defeated and what's left of your people will worship us. Before then I will grind your bones to dust."

"Dr. Ryan, we've heard enough of this nonsense. Administer the anesthesia now," Mullins ordered.

"With pleasure," Dr. Ryan said, as she turned up the sedation and stared down the captive.

As Tamir-Benob drifted back to sleep he smiled and spoke loudly in Hebrew, "I will kill you all."

Dr. Ryan shuddered at Uri's translation and watched the giant pass out. "Not if we have anything to say about it, you beast," she promised.

*⟫⟫ ⟪⟪*

For the rest of the day, Subject Alpha remained heavily sedated and under constant surveillance. Heightened security levels had made it difficult for the turncoat to be alone with the subject. The opportunity to become excessively wealthy and participate in global dominance overcame his loyalty. The trick was to blend in, which had taken more time than expected. Hidden by late night monitoring responsibilities, he waited for the chance to bring the patient from a general anesthesia level to a more minimal sedation level—that would allow Alpha to escape the compound.

Slight reductions in anesthesia would be less noticeable over time, and disarming alarms would be necessary to keep staff members unaware of the changes. No one would be monitoring respiratory rates, oxygen saturation, and other vitas for the next hour. This should provide adequate time for Alpha to awake. After modifying the data logs, the discrete agent left the detention cell.

---

As night approached, Gunther was observant while he spoke to Klaus van Wilhelm, the vice chair of the Council of Five.

"How are the preparations coming along?" van Wilhelm asked.

"They are complete, and we are near the US military compound. The men are anxious but ready for the encounter," Gunther answered with determination.

"Excellent. The council will be pleased. Capturing the subject is priority and will require perfect execution before their military can intervene. Our head start on the Americans is our only advantage. Do your best but ensure the integrity of the DNA samples, as that is our number one priority. Make sure you bring the American contact with you. That is critical to our future success."

"Understood. We have prepared for this moment, and ready." Gunther replied.

"Keep us posted of progress."

As Gunther hung up, he smiled, as the big men knew their goals were one step closer. Besides riches, he would be chosen as one to have longevity. He would be a true superman, a king among the rest of humankind.

Thoughts of the possibilities raced through Klaus van Wilhelm's mind as he ended the call. They were closer than ever before. As vice chair of the council, he helped lead a consortium of super wealthy families from several European countries. The Council of Five had existed for over one hundred years and had shaped policy in Europe. The group was organized like a military unit, with tentacles in government, religion, banking, and even the infamous Bilderberg Group.

The council had been temporarily sidelined during World War II with Hitler's rise in Germany. Some of his leaders dabbled in the occult and collected religious artifacts. Fortunately, the Nazi movement was run by a bunch of zealots who couldn't appreciate the significance of the objects related to the Nephilim in their possession. The council slowly managed to steal the Nazi's secrets about the fallen and their children prior to their defeat.

As one of the leaders of the council, van Wilhelm's aristocrat family had ties to Europe going back a thousand years, which was a prerequisite for leadership. The Oxford education prepared him to take his place in the organization, just like his father had done. So many connections, all leading back to a central point in history.

Medical research into genetics was the recent venture of the group—more like their passion. There was ownership in pharmaceutical and biotech companies, of course, but their recent emphasis was genetic engineering and longevity. Multiple Nobel winners were on their pay roll or serving as paid consultants through complex holding companies. They also had the ability to monitor clandestine activities in various parts of the world. Any time the Chinese or North Koreans made secretive advancements the council always had inside people to pass along their learnings. Their group would be the first to benefit from new medicines and human enhancements, including this once-in-a-lifetime opportunity thanks to the Americans. The council would do anything to obtain this discovery.

As he enjoyed the water view from his Munich villa, van Wilhelm started a Zoom call with others on the council.

As Stone completed his late-night rounds, he studied the sheer size of Subject Alpha. The beast was built like the perfect predator. Stone was still amazed at how something so large could be real, with modern medicine suggesting this creature's existence should not be possible.

There was eye movement. That can't be happening he thought. Stone checked some of the vitals, they were off. He noticed Tamir-Benob's heart rate and breathing had increased from earlier. Stone quickly called two others for backup.

"Get Dr. Mullins on the horn. We have a red alert," he shouted.

Tamir-Benob was slowly waking from the anesthesia. He had an increased awareness of those in the room. As his arms and legs grew stronger, he considered opening his eyes completely and sitting up. His enhanced hearing allowed him to distinguish their pleas for reinforcements from other sounds in the room. The more he listened, the quicker he learned their language. The time for escape was now.

As Stone stood exhausted in the room, he looked on in disbelief as Subject Alpha sat up and eyed him as a predator assesses their prey.

"Get the others here!" yelled a shocked Stone.

Before the soldiers could move, Subject Alpha snapped his chains and ripped the shackles off his legs. He grabbed the nearest soldier with one hand and threw him against the wall, snapping his neck and killing him instantly.

Stone fired his MK 17 SCAR-H heavy duty weapon with 7.6 mm caliber at the beast. Subject Alpha was quick moving and avoided the bullets coming his way.

The oversized man picked up an IV pole, ripped out the needle in his arm, and speared a nearby soldier. Tamir-Benob rushed the exit as Stone tried to close the cell door to block him from leaving. If Subject Alpha escaped, it would be a disaster.

Both Dr. Ryan and Dr. Mullins heard the alarm go off in their separate quarters and raced toward the containment cell.

"What's going on? Don't tell me he escaped?" an unbelieving Dr. Ryan asked.

"Don't know yet, but that better not be the case." replied Dr. Mullins.

Tamir-Benob made his way through the facility like a tornado, destroying expensive research equipment and knocking things over as he advanced outward. Several soldiers challenged him as he approached the staircase. The bullets stung and would take time to heal. An aggressive soldier approached him with a large knife and stabbed for his stomach. The giant caught his arm, breaking it and taking the knife away. He stabbed the soldier with his own knife, lifting him off the ground, before he continued his march to exit the facility. He left a bloody trail in his wake.

As Mullins and Ryan ran into Stone, they demanded an update.

"Stone, what's the status? Where is the subject?"

"I noticed eye movement and increased heart rate and respiration. But just as I called for backup, he broke free," Stone quickly explained. "There was no indication the anesthesia was wearing off. We couldn't contain him. I've never seen anything so strong. He took several slugs and just kept moving. There are multiple casualties, and the first response team has been activated to capture him. The subject is moving toward the north exit, and troops will be engaging shortly."

"I told you this would happen, Colonel Mullins!" Dr. Ryan yelled, unable to contain her exasperation. "We may not be able to stop him. You should have sent him to a more secure facility. The blood is on your hands. We can't let him into the civilian population! There will be many more deaths if that happens."

"We *are* going to stop him," Mullins corrected her.

Tamir-Benob continued to make his way toward the exit. Smoke filled the room from the gunfire, and some of the facility's power had been lost due to the damage. He had been shot multiple times, and the blood loss from his wounds was slowing him down. He needed to feed and rest.

There were more soldiers approaching. He threw a heavy piece of office equipment, surprising the first soldier and crushing his upper torso. Other soldiers opened fire. He deflected some of the bullets with a piece of scrap metal he had picked up along the way. He quickly advanced on the remaining soldiers and killed each one with little effort, leaving multiple dead bodies strewn across the floor. The room looked like a war zone, and the smoke and small fires from the gunfire made it difficult to see. Wanting to keep moving, he made his way for the exit door and freedom.

Tamir-Benob felt alive again as he left the complex. This was his first time outdoors since his capture and his senses exploded all at once as he breathed in the fresh air. The wind blew through his hair; the morning chill felt invigorating as his feet finally touched the grass. Lush vegetation surrounded him—it was so much greener than the desert he was used to. He saw mountains with snow in the backdrop. *Surely there would be caves and plenty of wild game.* It reminded him of his early homeland near Philistia and Mount Hermon. The sun would be rising soon, and he would need to move quickly to avoid detection. He started off in a trot and left the military compound under the cover of darkness, carrying the bloodied IV pole as a weapon in one hand.

꘎꘎꘎꘎ ꘎꘎꘎꘎

As Mullins and his security team made their way to the facility entrance, they passed several bodies. It appeared that one soldier may have been a victim of a cannibalistic attack. The surface door had been ripped off its hinges and thrown aside. There was no sign of Subject Alpha; he was long gone, but tracks led away from the facility.

"Colonel, the tracks head toward the mountains on the Crow reservation. The footprints are huge, and stride length is more than double that of a typical human male," observed one of the lab techs nearby.

"Stone, get a team together and go after that thing. We can't let him get too far." A frustrated Mullins ordered. "I will update the General and get reinforcements here. Time is critical." As Stone left, Mullins contemplated what he would tell General Briggs.

A short time later, Mullins made the dreaded call to his superior. Obtaining permission to send troops on to American Indian land was proving to be a headache.

"General, Subject Alpha has escaped, and there are several casualties. He's heading on to the Crow Reservation. Drones have been activated as we speak to try and find him."

"Mullins, you assured me this would not happen. This is a damn disaster!" General Briggs shouted into the phone. "The president will need to be notified, and he may have to implement the Insurrection Act to mobilize troops on civilian land. He will hate that. And if we activate troops of any kind, including the National Guard, that will involve the governor and a lot of fall out. Have you called the state police?"

"Stone is handling that. They're creating a perimeter to keep the locals out and are evacuating the general public. We're telling the civilians that an experimental drug had a side effect and that an escaped military test subject had an adverse reaction and we're searching for him. The perimeter is wide enough that the state police shouldn't see anything. The cover story is working so far," Mullins explained.

"For the Crow Reservation, we'll need to go through Indian Affairs. I'll call the cabinet head and include the local tribal IA law enforcement group. Heaven help us if this thing gets far into the mountains or onto the reservation and we can't find him. That would mean a lot of civilian casualties—and your assignment to a remote post for the rest of your career."

"Understood. In the interim, can you send more security and troops to help track the subject?" Mullins asked, his desperation showing despite his best effort.

"Yes, but it will be a couple of hours before they arrive. You will need to handle this with the resources at hand till then. How soon before Stone goes after him?"

"Stone is preparing to go out at daybreak in the next hour. We will get him back."

"You had better get him back." And with out another word hung up.

As daybreak was encroaching on the military post, contact was made with the Council of Five by the undercover American agent.

"Yes?" an enthusiastic van Wilhelm sounded as he answered the call.

"The creature has escaped as we planned. Several soldiers were killed, and he took several bullet wounds, so he is weakened."

"Ah, but a wounded, cornered animal is always more dangerous. And the samples?" van Wilhelm asked.

"The samples are safe and secured. I gave them to your currier. The arrival of the DNA should be on schedule. The US military will send more troops later today, but your men have a head start by a couple of hours. Drones are searching for the beast now, but the dense foliage will keep him hidden most likely."

"Do you know the direction he was heading?"

"Southwest toward one of the mountain ranges, the Pryor mountains. He has had time to travel approximately five kilometers away from here by now."

# Chapter Five

# Sounding the Alarm at the Reservation

**W**HITMAN ANSWERED HIS PHONE **groggily as the** 4:30 a.m. clock light flashed in front of him.

"Agent Whitman? This is dispatch."

"This better be important."

"There are reports of heavy gunfire and explosions near the military research base. Tribal members are calling in frantic. We called you first."

"Ok, I'll check it out. Have the team go on standby."

His thoughts wandered to the recent reports of helicopters flying overhead and wondered if something worse was occurring.

After a quick weapons check he was out the door before sunrise toward the outskirts of the reservation.

Following hot coffee and a drive down dark roads, he pulled into the military research facility and was stopped at the state patrol checkpoint.

"Straight ahead, agent. The officer in charge should be near the tent outside the building."

As he parked his vehicle, he was approached by a large well-built man dressed in all black carrying a full gamut of armament.

"I'm Harold Stone, head of the security team overseeing this facility, and who are you?" Two very serious men flanked Stone, hands on rifles, with live ammunition.

Whitman wondered why a private contract security company was needed for a low-grade military medical research facility. His prior military service suggested these types of teams were used in unusual situations, especially if you were trying to conceal something.

Whitman showed his badge and forcefully stated, "Special Agent Frank Ironhorse Whitman of Indian Affairs. I received calls from concerned Crow members regarding gunfire. Given the proximity to Crow land, I need to know what's going on and what risk there is to those on the reservation." Whitman purposely withheld information, waiting to see if the security agent would tip his hand.

Stone sized him up and asked, "Special Agent Whitman, you look like former military?"

"Yes, Third Ranger Battalion out of Fort Benning."

"Rangers lead the way, Special Agent. I served with the Second Battalion out of Washington State."

"So, what can you tell me, Stone?"

"What we are at liberty to say is that a special test subject under an experimental drug treatment escaped, is considered dangerous, and is being tracked by the military. We want to minimize any contact with the civilian population. The state police are setting up a perimeter to keep civilians out of danger."

Whitman consciously noted the helicopter landing pad nearby and put two and two together.

"You have a heavy state patrol presence and soldiers walking around the base of operations with live ammo on US soil. How dangerous is the subject? More than civilian authorities can handle?" Whitman asked. "Why would the military perform a risky experiment out here and not a main military facility with better security? Seems like an odd location for an experimental drug with military soldiers, if that was the only thing being tested."

Stone paused for a second before answering. "Yes, more dangerous since the test subject is highly trained; but we are here to provide security, not make command decisions on why and where experiments are conducted."

No give from Stone, so Whitman tried again. "I know the drill, and you're not telling me much, so can we get the officer in charge here to speak with me?"

"Yes, I've already called Lieutenant Colonel Mullins."

Whitman waited impatiently for Mullins, knowing the officer's arrival was being delayed on purpose.

Mullins was anticipating the conversation with the Indian Affairs agent since they were so close to the Crow Indian Reservation. General Briggs had spoken to the interior secretary, the cabinet member overseeing Indian Affairs. He had approval to bring the military onto reservation land, but this was a tenuous subject. The president expected blowback, but it would be easier to deal with it after the fact.

Mullins was given Whitman's name and military history before their meeting and was hopeful that as a former special operations soldier Whitman could help handle the delicate situation. Mullins had asked Captain Ryan to join in and eyed Whitman as they approached the security station.

"Agent Whitman, I'm Lieutenant Colonel Mullins, and the officer in charge. This is my associate Captain Kathryn Ryan. We're both physicians leading the research teams. You surely have questions, and we can share some information, but a lot of this is classified top secret."

Whitman studied both military officers. They were dressed in standard army fatigues. Mullins was a tall, stern, gaunt-looking man in his late fifties, with a grey receding hairline. His glasses gave him a scholarly look. Ryan, mid-thirties, tall and slender with long, straight, red hair and bright green eyes. She had a fiery look. Whitman was good at reading people, and there was much more here than they were letting on.

"Thank you, Dr. Mullins and Dr. Ryan," Whitman said, choosing to use their medical titles. "What can you tell me about the current situations? How much risk is there to the members of the Crow reservation? Mr. Stone has already confirmed a test subject has escaped. Why would you be experimenting on human subjects, and what type of work were you doing?"

"We are not at liberty to discuss the type of medical research, but the escaped subject is very dangerous. The area needs to be cordoned off, and the military should handle this," Mullins replied.

"What are you talking about—a soldier on steroids or some sort of super drug? I need to know what we're facing in case the test subject ends up on reservation land. Can one escaped man really justify this type of manhunt? What are you not telling me?"

Mullins hesitated a few seconds and then answered grimly. "The subject has enhanced strength, is very large and fast moving, and because of his enhancements, normal bullets only slow him down. That's why we're asking nonmilitary to let us handle this."

"Are you kidding me? How can bullets only slow a man down? What science experiment have you cooked up? I know you research types are always looking for ways to enhance soldiers. Tell me what's going on! My people are going to be at risk."

"Agent, more troops are arriving soon, and they will capture the escaped subject. Keep members of the reservation outside the police perimeter. This is a national security issue, and Indian Affairs has ceded jurisdiction on tribal land. Local law enforcement is also cooperating. We'll make sure no one is at risk on the reservation. By tomorrow this should be resolved. I can't tell you more than that," Mullins stated.

"I don't believe you, Dr. Mullins. Why would you need more troops, what happened to the soldiers on post? The damage here is significant. I don't believe national security is required for a medical research facility. I'll be calling the Bureau of Indian Affairs and will activate our own law enforcement team to protect members of the reservation who are at risk from this fiasco. Stone, are you settling for this?"

"Agent Whitman, the escapee will be captured," a defiant Stone replied.

Whitman stared at him a long time waiting for more.

Dr. Ryan looked away in disgust. She agreed with the agent. Innocent people would probably die because of the secrecy and deception. She was torn between duty and morality and wanted to tell Whitman the truth.

As Stone escorted Whitman back to his vehicle, he knew he was being played. He clearly wasn't going to get anywhere here.

꘎꘎꘎

Gunther and the commando team waited anxiously near the military base to begin their mission. They had heard the noisy firefight nearby and knew the creature had escaped and was likely only a few miles from their location.

Gunther felt his phone vibrate in his jacket pocket. "Gunther are you there?" a voice inquired.

"Yes, the line is secure."

"You have a green light. Coordinates of the last sighting and direction of the target have been sent to your GPS. A handful of US Army Rangers from the facility are preparing to search now. Most were killed during the creature's escape. It may be useful to let the Rangers engage first and then approach—although that is your tactical decision. The target has left the military grounds and is traveling toward nonmilitary areas and the Indian reservation as planned. There may be other local police officers and tribal law enforcement called in by now, so discretion is important. Try to minimize civilian casualties, but we can't let loss of life deter us from mission success."

"Understood. We will be departing in less than five minutes. And the samples?" Gunther asked.

"They have been handed off to our courier and are being sent directly to our lab in Germany."

"Excellent. And our internal acolyte for the mission? Still alive?"

"Yes, alive and needed to help accelerate our timeline. You have a picture and should look to make contact, when possible, over the next few hours to arrange departure with your team."

"I will update as we make progress. Gunther out."

❦

As Whitman got into his car, Dr. Ryan stepped up to his car and quickly placed a small piece of paper through his window. He had not seen her slip discreetly away from the group.

"Agent Whitman, I can't speak to you here, but meet me at this location in one hour and I'll explain what's going on. There's something evil happening, and you need to know the truth," she said.

Whitman took the slip of paper from Dr. Ryan. "A little dramatic, don't you think? I appreciate the help, but why are you telling me this? This will get you in hot water."

"A horrible wrong is transpiring, and if you're going to help stop this, you need to know what you're up against. Lives are at stake. I'm not sure if anyone can stop it. I can't say anything else here, but I can tell you more later." She slowly disappeared toward the facility and away from the sight of the others.

❦

Gunther plotted the direction the giant was heading based on recent GPS coordinates. Their quarry was heading toward Big

Pryor Mountain, known for its ice caves and tall mountain peaks, located on the American Indian reservation.

"Giovanni, it looks like we can intercept the beast near Chief Plenty Coups State Park before he gets too far into the mountains," Gunther suggested.

"Si, we will arrange for a low flyby to stay below radar. The drone feeds will help us narrow his location," Giovanni assured his leader.

"Make sure everyone is locked and loaded. Plan to use tranquilizer darts if possible. If not, the specimen will still be valuable brought in dead."

The men quickly loaded the chopper and took off toward the area where the giant was last seen.

***

Ryan arrived at the coffee shop before Whitman. The shop was scattered between other businesses about five miles from the military post. She was cautious, afraid she might have been followed by the military. Fortunately, Mullins was preoccupied with getting Stone out to track the giant and didn't notice her slip away. Just to be safe she parked behind the building to conceal her vehicle. She wore civilian clothes and a hat to blend in with the public.

The coffee shop was busy, as the early morning crowd was beginning to arrive. After grabbing a couple of drinks, she went back outside to wait for Whitman. She watched nervously as

Whitman pulled up and quickly scanned the parking lot to ensure no one was watching them. She was beginning to have serious doubts on who to trust.

Ryan waved Whitman down as he walked toward the shop. She handed him a cup of java and said, "Let's keep walking, better to be safe that no one is eavesdropping."

"Why the cloak and dagger? Tell me what's going on," Whitman said as they crossed the parking lot together.

"I'm about to tell you something classified. You won't believe me, but you need to know because of the danger involved."

"Ok, you have my attention."

"The test subject we were holding is not a US military test subject taking a drug. It's a captured beast from the mountains in a remote part of the world."

"Beast, like a large animal?"

"No, not an animal, a large hybrid man, that speaks, is super intelligent, and is difficult to injure."

"A tribesman?"

"No, a giant man over ten feet tall with red hair. This sounds like a made-up story, but it's not. His biology is not human. I tried to slow things down with the military, warn them of the danger, but they wouldn't listen. Their goal was to wake him, and now he has escaped after killing many soldiers."

"Dr. Ryan—"

"Call me Kathryn."

"Kathryn, I have a hard time believing this. Why in the world would a creature like that be at the lab in the first place?" Whitman inquired.

She continued to look around franticly hoping they were not being watched. A slow traveling black sedan caught her attention momentarily.

"My line of research is improving soldier readiness through biological augmentation—a good cause, to protect our troops. We thought we could learn from this experiment, and the lab is placed in a remote location to keep this type of research secret from the general public," Dr. Ryan explained, looking down to avoid Whitman's eyes. She was disgusted by how all this sounded.

"A super soldier program. Rumors of this type of experimentation were going on when I served. It's morally reprehensible, but I'm not surprised at the extent our government goes to."

"Morality aside, intelligence from local tribesman documented this creature's existence. They were terrified of him, and even the Taliban avoided him. He's not a normal man as we know, and not a product of an experiment. An extraction team brought him in after a firefight in the mountains. He appears to be incredibly old, maybe a thousand years, with the strength of several men. We found old texts in the cave, and the archaeologist involved claimed the giant was a child of the famed Watchers or fallen angels from Genesis 6 in the Bible. I saw him rip handcuffs off and break the wrist of a large man effortlessly. We barely contained him. He killed over fifteen capable special operations soldiers during his escape, all while taking several high caliber bullet wounds. He's more than dangerous; I would call him an unstoppable force of nature."

"Do you expect me to believe this? This sounds like a fairy tale, Kathryn. This is even more weird than the strange stuff I experienced during my time in the Middle East."

"You have to believe me and take this seriously, Agent Whitman."

"You can call me Frank, but you lost me at giant."

"What kind of creature would it take to kill a team of highly trained Army Rangers? Because if he's successful in reaching civilian territory, things may get even worse," Dr. Ryan stated.

"Why is that?"

Ryan was visibly frightened. "After we woke him, he threatened to kill all of us. He boasted that there were more of his kind, and he was going to wake them and start a holy war against mankind."

"There are others of his kind? This is beginning to sound like our tribal legends from hundreds of years ago," Whitman muttered. "Was this thing transported a few nights ago to the base on a helicopter in the dead of night?"

"Yes, I helped supervise his arrival. A stealth team brought him in after they arrived in the States. We met the team when they landed on the base. And as far as others, I haven't seen any of his kind, but Dr. Mullins referenced once in conversation that there were reports of others in various parts of the Middle East."

Whitman's reply came with noticeable disgust. "If such a creature existed, why would you think you could control it? The military gave no thought as to how this would impact others. This creature will make its way toward reservation land to use the cover of the mountains, creating a problem for my people."

"We truly thought we could contain it. We had a chance opportunity with this creature, and we had to take it," Ryan answered with remorse in her voice.

"That's always the way of the military, trying to maximize every situation without thinking through the consequences, of the civilians they're putting at risk while they play with forces beyond their control. I just pray that no one else dies, especially members of the Crow tribe. My people are in immense danger now. I have to go." As Whitman left alone to contemplate things.

He could see the lights of the military base in the distance as he stopped to rest. Tamir-Benob had made fast time, with almost unlimited endurance. Ahead he saw the mountains—his ultimate destination and a reminder of home. Caves would be a good place to hide, and he would feed off the land like he had always done.

He would face a battle with man, as that was his destiny, and he looked forward to it. If there were others like him, an alliance would need to be made.

The sun would rise soon. A small settlement lay ahead, and the scent of man was nearby. He would be able to rest and feed again. A cautious approach was best until he could assess the number of warriors present.

⟶⟫⟫  ⟪⟪⟵

Gunther's team was using thermal imaging cameras and drones to track the creature. They had a head start on the military and knew he was heading toward the Pryor Mountains. The seven commandoes were handpicked for this mission. The Council of Five had a small archeological and nonhuman research team working the past several years to identify the possibility of hybrid human beings and how to apply their genetics to humans. There were multiple locations around the globe that had promising leads, but this find was rather unexpected.

Something big came up on their camera. It was too large to be a bear or wild horse. First contact! All were instantly alert. They would find a starting point and approach the creature on foot.

Tamir-Benob heard a noise overhead, awakening him from a brief nap. It was a large mechanical flying bird, and his instinct told him it was dangerous. He had seen these before, as they flew warriors who hunted him in the past. Most likely this was from the facility that had held him captive. He could bring the flying bird down but would bide his time and wait in ambush.

~·≫⫸ ⫷≪·~

Mullins was putting out several fires at once. General Briggs wanted a minute-by-minute accounting. More special operations troops were on their way but would not arrive for a few hours—enough time for major damage by Subject Alpha. Mullins had a skeleton security team that was preparing to leave to track the escaped subject. Finally, there was work to do with the local authorities to warn the public and prevent a major political disaster.

"General, we have our Ranger team leaving now. Drones are trying to track the subject. We're evacuating the area and creating a wide perimeter to avoid civilian casualties."

"This needs to be contained. The president spoke with cabinet officials to keep things concealed for the moment, and they're working through Indian Affairs. Expect media to flock to the area before long. We'll send a public relations expert to your location to help with the press. Keep me in the loop every minute. Understood, Colonel?"

"Yes, Sir." Mullins still believed they could contain this. He finished the call and left to find Stone before his team set out to track Subject Alpha.

After his call with Mullins, Briggs used his nonmilitary issued cell phone to call his contact.

"Briggs here. We're dealing with the problem. Once we capture him, we'll go to stage two. Our inside man is obtaining samples from the North Carolina location. I'll keep the group updated as I have more information. Let's plan to convene in a few days when we know more."

After the call with General Briggs, Mullins found Stone in the weapons room as he was preparing to leave the base.

"Stone, I'm glad I caught you. I've spoken to the general, and he wants action now. When are you leaving?"

"We're heading out in five minutes. Subject Alpha is moving fast, so every minute is critical. We'll report in every fifteen minutes."

"Good. Bring him in alive if possible, but, if necessary, you have approval for termination."

"One way or another we will end this," Stone said and left to gather the team.

## Chapter Six

# Indian Affairs Plan to Capture the Military Test Subject

WHITMAN CALLED AN EARLY morning emergency briefing with his team along with a few volunteer members of his tribe. His supervisor had already received orders from the Department of Indian Affairs, which had heard from the Department of Interior. The official word was to evacuate people, and work with the state patrol. His boss agreed that tribal members were at risk. Because of the time it would take for the military to mobilize and the risk to those on the reservation, Whitman and a small team would track the escaped subject while others in the department worked on evacuation efforts. Whitman updated IA and military command. He then addressed his team.

"We have first blood with our adversary. It will get much worse before it gets better. Blackhawk, call the rest of our men and activate our emergency response protocol for the reservation. We need to move quickly to make up ground on the giant."

Most of Whitman's men were already gathered in the small room and were sipping on coffee. He could hear them talking amongst themselves as he rounded the corner, sure they would be skeptical of some the things he was about to say. Most had rumors of what they were up against.

"Good morning everyone," he said as a way to get their attention.

His second in command Jim Blackhawk was the first to speak up. "Ironhorse, this sounds like a fairy tale. Giants just do not exist. There is no credible proof."

"Normally I would agree Jim, but there's enough corroborating evidence that we have a bad situation in play. You've received calls yourself that there are clandestine military helicopters flying in the middle of the night. Now we've got heavy gunfire, several dead bodies, and at least one witness who is a military medical doctor. We have to assume this story is true and take it as a serious threat," Whitman iterated.

Mighty Eagle, the tribal elder, interjected with a voice of authority. "Everyone listen to me. This story sounds impossible in this day and age but let me remind you of what our fathers taught us about our ancestors."

The group went silent as the wise one continued to speak.

"Many moons ago, before the white man built up their large cities and became numerous in our lands, the Crow were mighty and hunted freely. This was over three hundred years ago when our people first came to this area near the mountains. The Crow battled a tribe of fierce pale-faced, red-haired warriors. In our crow language we called them *isshiia' hǐsshe bilaxpáakisaate* or red-haired giants. Some of these giants were said to be eleven to twelve feet tall, animal like, and rejected any offers of peace. They were stronger than our mightiest warriors, could withstand the cold, and lived in the caves, including the Great Ice Cave on our current reservation. Traditional Crow weapons were not able to stop these mighty men. For many years, the giants took our animals, kidnapped our women, and battled our warriors. It was said these giants were cannibalistic. We lost many of our people in the battles.

"Legends suggest the red hairs were half evil spirit and half man and had forbidden knowledge. This aligns with the Christian beliefs of fallen angels during the time of Noah the great Ark builder. Our people almost left this land due to this evil. As a last resort, our medicine men asked the Great Spirit for wisdom on how our warriors could rid the land of this evil. The mighty Crow gathered their bravest warriors for one last battle. Many died, but they managed to chase the last of the remaining giants to a cave with no exit. Several braves went into the cave to fight the beasts, and gave their lives to hold them at bay, while the others built a large roaring fire with soft, dry wood at the cave entrance. Any giants who did make it to the entrance of the cave were held back by Crow arrows and men who sacrificed themselves by diving into the fire to prevent their exit. As the fire burned, the tribe pushed the embers into the cave and closed it up with boulders. The smoke and heat killed the last of the giants along with the Crow warriors. Their death screams haunted our brothers for years."

Mighty Eagle took a somber pause and then continued his story. "For many years afterward, our people kept watch for a reoccurrence of these evil spirit men. That is why the story has been handed down for over ten generations to our people, lest we forget and evil returns. From what you have told us Ironhorse, the US military has brought this curse back to our land. We have a sacred duty to stop this, or all our people will be at risk."

"Mighty Eagle, I mean no disrespect, but how can this escaped creature be the same as in our legends?" a young Indian affairs officer respectfully asked.

"It may not be, but there is much similarity to our legends. Our history says the giant palefaces were here at the time our people settled here and that they may have migrated from across the ocean. The escaped creature from the military base is incredibly old and sounds much like our legends. It is unlikely the similarities are by chance. How many stories do you hear of eleven-foot-tall half spirit lalf men? Most likely this creature was a remnant of the early group who migrated to our lands.

Remember, these were creatures with great power, who lived much longer than man, and were able to travel great distances quickly. Since our ancestors believed these super men were endowed with bad spirits, they thought it would take powerful magic to battle them. Many cultures have reported beings such as these, so they all may be rooted in a common origin."

Ironhorse looked around the room with determination. "Listen to the words of Mighty Eagle and take this seriously. Regardless of the origin, this will be the most dangerous mission you go on. Treat this operation with extreme seriousness. The IA team and three Crow warriors will accompany me to track the creature. There is a small US military team tracking now, and the state patrol is forming a perimeter. Everyone else will work to evacuate tribal members as discussed, especially those in a fifty-mile radius of Pryor, Montana. We believe the giant is probably avoiding larger population areas and heading toward mountains, given his habitat. The IA communications center is activated, and we'll stay connected every fifteen to thirty minutes. Be ready to leave in a few minutes."

As daylight shined through the trees, Gunther and his team fast roped down from the helicopter and hit the ground running. They were in camouflage colors to try and blend into their surroundings.

The giant had been on the loose for a few hours and had already traveled several miles away from the base. They were less than a half mile from their last thermal image of their target. The subject was moving much faster than a normal human. They would plan to tranquilize the creature, load it into the helicopter, and take it to an awaiting truck for transport.

Tamir-Benob doubled back around and used the heavy dense trees to conceal his approach. The mercenaries were advancing in stealth, but his preternatural vision allowed him to see them far ahead. Their scent gave them away as well. He positioned himself high in a large tree and waited. The foliage provided cover from prying eyes until it would be too late to see him.

Giovanni felt uneasy and gripped his semi-automatic rifle tightly. The hair on the back of his neck stood up, as he quietly moved through the brush. He was in the point position, stepping softly, as two others trailed behind him. They had lost the giant moments ago but were near his last location.

With a crash the red-haired beast leapt out of the trees between Giovanni and his men. The size of the hybrid man shocked the seasoned team before they could fire.

Tamir-Benob speared one of the men through the heart against a tree with the IV pole, quickly killing him. Then with a quick motion, the giant threw a knife he had taken from a former kill, striking a second commando between the eyes.

Giovanni lowered his rifle and fired, hitting the giant center mass with a large force, but only slowing him down.

Tamir-Benob yelled in pain and disappeared into the brush at inhuman speed.

Gunther quickly appeared with a squad of men. Horrified at the sight of the two dead team members, he voiced a cry for vengeance.

"Giovanni, we have to keep moving, he is just ahead of us," he shouted.

"I hit him dead center and he shrugged it off and kept going," Giovanni murmored in disbelief.

In the distance Whitman heard rifle shots. His team was a few miles from the base on the Crow Reservation tracking the giant. The military team couldn't have made it this far. The IA communications team confirmed his suspicions. Another team was engaging the escaped subject. This could be trouble, and possibly mean more deaths.

Whitman and his team mounted their horses and took off toward the noise. One of his men had brought along an American Indian dog, similar to a Siberian Husky. The dog, Scout, would give them an advanced warning if they were attacked. They studied the footprints leading away from the compound and continued onward toward the city of Pryor, directly through the state park filled with campers. The state patrol was supposed to have evacuated the park, but there would always be holdouts, especially older tribesman.

If they did not catch this thing in the next few hours, it would make it to the mountains and caves and would be nearly impossible to capture. Their odds were low; they had to move faster.

The governor of Montana had been notified of the recent events and was unhappy that the White House and Indian Affairs kept this information concealed from the public. He wanted to declare a statewide emergency. Mullins had been able to convince the governor's team that things were under control, that danger was limited to the reservation, and that the state patrol along with military and Indian Affairs agents could handle it.

Mullins next problem was calming his staff down and repairing their containment cell to hold Subject Alpha for transport to Guantanamo Bay. Helicopters were on standby upstate at the air force base and could arrive quickly to provide transport He would be relieved if they could accomplish that. Dr. Ryan was becoming a challenge to manage, as she favored going public with the news, and it was becoming harder to convince her to help keep it all under wraps and that what they were doing was for the greater good.

Stone and his team were having little success in tracking Subject Alpha. His trail had gone cold. They had come across some tracks, but they ended near a stream. The beast must have entered the stream to throw them off. The overhead drones had not provided additional information, and they were running out of time. His team was on the outer edges of the state park but closer to Pryor. Ahead were the Stratford Hills, an open area at an elevation of over five thousand feet.

"Uri lets break the team into two smaller groups and head in the opposite directions to try and flush him out. Keep in close contact," Stone instructed.

⤜⤜⤜ ⤛⤛⤛

Tamir-Benob tracked the mercenaries through the forest. Several men were left after his first encounter. They were moving quietly in the wooded area, but he was downwind tracking by scent. He changed directions and approached two of his quarry from the rear. The soldiers were surprised when he rose from behind a large set of brush and punched the first man. The blow was hard enough to knock him backward into a nearby tree instantly killing him. The second mercenary started to speak, but the giant quickly grabbed him by the neck and crushed his windpipe, throwing his body aside like a rag doll. Tamir-Benob continued tracking the remaining men silently.

Gunther noticed two of his men were missing. They stopped to wait on the others, and the lack of sound in the forest gave him pause. Something was wrong, and he felt like they had become the prey and were no longer the hunters.

"Giovanni, when was the last contact with Hans and Stephano?" Gunther asked.

"About seven minutes ago, and they were approximately fifty yards to our rear. They are two minutes past check in time," a worried Giovanni stated.

Tamir-Benob had found a large boulder near the creek that ran nearby. It weighed over one-hundred pounds, but he carried it easily and prepared to use it as a projectile. He ran to where the remaining soldiers were resting and lobbed the boulder over his head at the nearest man, crushing him under its weight. A nearby commando raised his rifle to shoot, but the giant tore the weapon from his hands and used the tip to impale him. Startled by the speed of the beast, Gunther managed to get a few shots off.

Tamir-Benob howled in pain as he saw the blood flow from his wounds. He shouted a warning in English through snarling teeth. "Blood from you! Your transgression will be paid in full."

Giovanni lunged with a knife and struck the giant's leg. This only intensified Tamir-Benob's anger, and he swung wildly, barely missing him. Momentum from the missed swing carried the giant into the path of the last man. The Nephilim picked up the soldier with one hand and held him like a shield against Gunther's shots as he ran away. When he'd put enough distance between himself and the heavy gunfire, Tamir-Benob tossed the dead man aside.

Still in shock and disbelief at the size of the red-headed adversary, Gunther looked at Giovanni and noted the obvious, "Time to leave. Nothing will be gained by pursuing him now."

Giovanni agreed, and they took off hurriedly in the opposite direction of the beast.

※※※　※※※

After the encounter with the mercenaries, Tamir-Benob traveled a few more miles toward the mountains before resting. He had traveled to the outskirts of the state park, about thirty miles from the base. There were shelters by man built here, although he could not sense humans nearby.

It was midmorning, and he had fed on roots and berries and rested a few hours as his wounds began to heal. From his estimates he was heading in a southwest direction, and the mountains were less than a day's travel. They would provide the cover required. The soldiers nearby were different than the ones he faced during his earlier encounter, and he could smell the gun powder from their firesticks.

※※※　※※※

Dr. Ryan was back at the base speaking with Dr. Mullins about next steps in the event that Subject Alpha was captured.

"The team is ready for Subject Alpha if he's captured, but I need to go out and help supervise the efforts. I could help subdue the subject quicker and with less chance of injury to others," pushing hard to join the hunt.

Dr. Mullins thought for a moment. "That would be a dangerous approach. Although, someone should be there to make sure he's brought in uninjured and as you suggest, to prevent injuries to our troops."

"What if we took security with us for added protection?" Dr. Ryan asked.

"I'll consent if we both go, and if we take a security personnel with us. If he's captured the extraction team will be there as well."

"Let me gather a few medical items, and I'll meet you here in thirty minutes."

"Perfect. I'll arrange the security detail and transport. We'll go to the state park near where Stone and his team are currently tracking. See you shortly."

Stone and his team picked up Subject Alpha's tracks after several hours of searching. The second team came back to continue tracking as one unit. They were close; he could feel it. The Pryor Mountains were just on the outskirts of the park nearby. The area was remote, and few traveled here. The foliage made it difficult to see; it was an ideal location for an ambush. Stone heard twigs snapping, and then Subject Alpha appeared out of nowhere like a warrior god. His appearance was larger than when he had been in captivity, like a large colossus moving toward them. The hulking man carried spears in each arm and quickly threw them, hitting the two soldiers nearest Stone.

"Take cover!" yelled Stone.

"You!" Tamir-Benob said, pointing to Stone. "You tried to kill me in the containment area. I will fight you last, after watching your men die." He spoke in simple sentences and was learning English quickly.

The goliath disappeared behind a tree as the men took cover. He moved quickly, covering the distance faster than anyone should. Rapid gunfire erupted. Screams of men fighting for their life lingered as limbs were torn off.

Stone listened in horror as his men were killed. He ran toward the screams, only to find dead bodies and blood. There was no movement, no one left alive.

"Face me you coward. Stop killing my men!" Stone yelled.

Out of the corner of his eye, he saw the giant rush toward him. He swung his rifle in a fit of rage and hit the titan in the head, but it barely slowed him down. The behemoth pushed Stone hard, sending him sailing through the air. He landed hard. As Stone tried to stand, a sharp pain radiated through his lungs—a broken rib made it difficult to rise or even to breathe.

Tamir-Benob laughed as he looked down on the beaten soldier. "Is this all the fight you have in you, little man? You cannot prevent me from escaping."

Stone spit blood and stood to his feet. "Take this." He pulled out his Glock and fired multiple rounds into the chest of the giant, center mass with tissue smoldering. This should have been enough to put down a large man.

Tamir-Benob went to one knee and screamed in rage. "Your fire weapon will not save you." His ribs had been fractured by the steel and hurt to the touch. "I will enjoy killing you."

Whitman and a handful of his team had been tracking on foot due to the dense foliage. He knew these woods better than most, having grown up here near the mountains. They picked up their pace when they heard noise ahead. The US military unit was nearby, but they would probably need his team's help. They quietly made their way through the woods until they saw bloody soldiers scattered nearby. It looked like a massacre and was much worse than he had anticipated.

Whitman heard the muffled noise of a conversation up ahead. Scout issued a low growl, and Whitman gave a sign to hold the dog back to avoid giving away the element of surprise. It was clear now they did not have enough men to subdue the subject.

Stone knew he was about to die. "You can kill me, but I'm taking you with me," Stone shouted defiantly.

The Nephilim stood up straight, looking like a Greek god, and triumphantly walked toward Stone ready for the final kill. The earth shook as the massive executioner got closer, knife in hand.

Just then Whitman stepped into the clearing. His hardened demeanor and determined look momentarily drew their attention. He was a reminiscence of a deity of the forest. Time seemed to stand still, if only for a few seconds.

Tamir-Benob studied Whitman. He had the image of a warrior, strong jawline, and absolute determination. His red skin color contrasted with the others. There was no fear in this one. They locked eyes, warrior to warrior. Tamir-Benob was reminded of the young Israeli king thousands of years ago—the warrior who hunted his kind and killed many, at the urging of the unspeakable Hebrew God. For the first time in ages, Tamir-Benob felt fear. He growled to mask his emotion.

Whitman was taken back by the sheer size of the large human-looking ogre in front of him. The red-haired man thing was standing near an injured Stone, making him look small. Instinctively Whitman raised his Remington 870 shotgun and fired three rapid shots at the giant. Tamir-Benob's chest smoldered further, and he fell back struggling to stand. Although his chest pained him, he managed to hurl a nearby rock in response.

More Crow warriors and IA officers raised their weapons to fire on him. Scout ran forward barking and bit hard into the giant's arm. The dog was ferocious in his attack. With a howl, the giant grabbed the dog by the neck, held him as a shield, and ran into the bush, bleeding and severely hurt. Two tribesmen ran after him as he tossed the wounded dog, but they could not keep up with his rapid pace.

Stone, trying to maintain his control, looked at Whitman and said, "Thanks for the backup. We lost most of our men to that thing. He moved fast, and it was hard to get a bead on him. He took all the firepower we had, and it barely slowed him down. We have to go after him."

"You're not going anywhere near him right now. One of my men will take you to the horses and then back to base for medical treatment. You need to be patched up. He's injured, so we can track him. Our men are better trackers than the military and will get to him first, especially since he's in Crow territory," Stated an in-charge Whitman.

Whitman turned and addressed one of his tribesman. Running Brave. "How is Scout doing? He's a trooper."

"Not great, but we can patch him up. I'll take him back with Stone and then rejoin the group near the mountain."

"Thank you, Running Brave. We'll meet you there. If Mighty Eagle can spare more warriors, bring them with you. Be safe on the journey and protect Stone."

The Crow warrior nodded and said goodbye in their native language as he helped Stone back through the brush.

# Chapter Seven

# Scheming in Europe

**W**HILE THE BEAST WAS being tracked in America, van Wilhelm sipped his brandy in front of a roaring fireplace. He was finishing up his conversation with the Chancellor in preparation for a meeting later that day with the rest of the council.

The mysterious Chancellor's family was the wealthiest of the council, and collectively the group had a net worth of several hundred billion euros and controlling interests in various multinational companies. They funded a small security force and many other interests. Their wealth gave them power to influence politics, religion, and world affairs. Their organization had influence with the Vatican and Christian Orthodox churches on multiple continents as well. Their main focus was on increasing life span and tissue regeneration, and their grand plans were to be at the top of the food chain when the real fallen angelic rulers returned.

Many sources confirmed their suspicions that there was a more advanced, more powerful life-form interacting with humanity, and it was only a matter of time before their emergence in the lives of all. If only the public knew what had been hidden from them for so long—that man, with all its might, stood little chance to defend itself from the planned spiritual attack—there would be mass pandemonium.

The council's religious and military sources had managed to obtain a copy of the recent parchment from the creature captured by US military forces. The US Army was franticly trying to keep a lid on this, and a more influential American group was beginning to emerge.

"Klaus, let's discuss information from the parchment," the Chancellor pressed.

"Our team believes that the subject is one of the hybrid Nephilim spoken about in the biblical Old Testament," van Wilhelm described. "You have seen pictures of him obtained during his capture, and his sheer size and strength matches up with legends of old. He also has features mentioned in the ancient texts, such as red hair, six digits on his hands and feet, and a double row of teeth. The Americans radiocarbon-dated the age of his self-history parchment at over two thousand years old. Assuming he is the author of the parchment, he claims to be the nephew of Goliath of Gath near Mount Hermon. That

THE GENESIS 6 PROJECT

would make him second generation from one of the fallen and most likely from post-flood incursion of angelic beings."

"That would be an amazing find. We need to obtain the parchment for ourselves, as the Americans will keep this highly confidential given the religious implications and general population."

"In the Book of Jubilees, his father would have been described as a first-generation giant, and he would be a second-generation Nephilim. He describes battling the Israeli King David and being driven from the land of Palestine. He chronicles his history of migrating eastward and battling kings from Persia and other regions."

"Do you believe this is an authentic parchment?" the Chancellor asked.

"I think the collaborating evidence from the Vatican and other sources from Africa as well as what we have seen during this encounter is physical proof of their existence and incursion in our world. According to our internal contact at the US base, during his escape he killed several highly skilled American soldiers and received multiple gunshot wounds, which did not slow him down. His body seems to have the ability to regenerate from most wounds. That would suggest something beyond human."

"Can we capture and control him? Is Gunther and team adequate then?"

"That remains to be seen. Capturing him will be difficult, but our team has a couple of hours lead time on the Americans.

The biggest issue is whether our men can get close enough to tranquilize him. We believe we have adequate security and a holding cell at our compound. Our team has been working months to build and test the facility. It would be ideal to question him. Gunther will let us know how practical that will be, but we have not been able to reach him the last few hours. Which obviously is not a good sign."

"If the worst happens and Gunther is killed and the hybrid escapes, where do we stand?"

"The DNA sample will arrive tomorrow, and we will be able to move forward as planned. Gunther's team is supposed to acquire the American scientist. The biggest issue is how well human tissue is modifiable with implanted hybrid DNA, or if we can create and control our own clone of the creature," van Wilhelm explained. "Our expert from the US thinks that at the minimum, certain human genes related to tissue recovery and aging can be modified with the hybrid DNA."

"Excellent. The council looks forward to learning more later today. Another question. Did he mention the Nazarene in any of his writings?" inquired the Chancellor.

"No, not directly. But he did mention his hatred for the Church, especially the Vatican and its emissaries. He equated King David and his descendants to forebearers of the current Christian Church. He also described the many skirmishes with the Knights Templar over the ages in Italy and France."

"Did the Vatican papers mention the Templar connections?"

"Yes, although not in detail. We did find accounts where they ran across these behemoths after the Crusades. There were many Templars killed, and part of the reason the Templars built strategic fortified castles was to provide defense when they tried to rid their regions of these hybrids."

"Any other groups of interest he interacted with?"

"There are references to skirmishes with Alexander the Great, various struggles with the Roman Empire including Maximinus Thrax, and more recently the Russian military forces. Once the US forces arrived as of late, he had fewer interactions. The only reason the American's found him in such a faraway place was their focus on terroism."

"Interesting. Where there any talismans found?"

"Outside his personal scroll, no. Many of his kind supposedly worshipped the Canaanite god Baal, but there is no mention of this in his parchment nor any religious artifacts. I do not think there is any sign of the dark arts or grimoires for ancient spells the Watchers were supposedly famous for, although he has superhuman physical abilities, including the ability to heal and regenerate from injuries quickly. We suspect he has heightened senses as well but cannot be sure yet. There were various weapons from victims in the cave dating back hundreds of years, and a few chalices, but nothing of significance. A few modern American firearms were found, but no trace of their bodies."

"We will learn much from this. The war will be coming soon. There will be no quarter for the week," the Chancellor said callously.

"I will keep you posted, Chancellor. Much will happen over the next two days. Our destiny is one step closer."

"Very good, Klaus."

⫸⫷

Gunther provided an update to van Wilhelm prior to his meeting with the full council. It was concerning that most of their men had been killed by the giant. This project was one of the most ambitious to date. Over the last five years they had set up several secret biological research laboratories and spent millions of euros. The central lab in Germany had collected samples from all across Europe, including churches, grave sites, and old texts. None of those activities had provided viable tissue samples.

"Fellow council members, we are making progress.

I sent an image of the creature from our contact at the base to everyone prior to this call. Appearance is just as told in the legends.

Since our last communication, we have obtained a DNA sample and the creature has escaped as planned. Unfortunately, Gunther and his team were not able to capture the specimen. He proved to be more formidable than anticipated. Most of the team were killed in the process. Highly disappointing."

"What happened to the team? Can you share more?" a council member asked.

100

"According to Gunther, the creature is slowed very little by bullets or knife wounds. He heals very quickly. Besides his size, he has superhuman strength and is very ferocious. The team confronted him, but he overpowered them. Fortunately, Gunther and Giovanni escaped. They will be making their way back here over the next couple of days once they have the US scientist.

"Excellent, and how soon before we can test with human subjects?" another council member asked.

"Our new lab director tells us they can accelerate the progress, but we don't know how long until they begin testing. The super genes must be identified first. But having the sample means we are one step closer. We will be able to accomplish our goal and will be that much closer to working with the fallen when they come back. Based on the history of the current specimen, our members will be strong and live thousands of years." van Wilhelm assured the group. The meeting continued, with excitement building with the council.

# Chapter Eight

# Encounter at Chief Plenty Coups State Park

**Dr. Mullins and Dr. Ryan had made it to the drop** point of the US military extraction team. They had not heard from Stone for some time, but soldiers were stationed with transport vehicles nearby for Subject Alpha. After inquiring with the guard soldiers, they decided to follow the trail of the team to look for any signs of activity. They used the last known coordinates and followed the trail until they were out of sight of the remaining soldiers. It was only an hour before sunset, and the pending nightfall was worrisome.

Tamir-Benob had been severely injured by the rifle fire from Whitman. He managed to find a place in the park to rest.

His body was recovering, but he needed protein to aid in his regeneration. A small wild boar would have to do. Cooked meat would be preferred, but given the need for discretion, he would consume the meat raw.

As he made his way to exit the park, he picked up the trail of the earlier group of men. The warrior was still on his mind, he wanted to find him and exert vengeance for today. This one was strong, and he would need to be patient when approaching him. There were too many men present to attack just yet.

Gunther and Giovanni were unaware they were being tracked by Tamir-Benob. Given the military presence, they had to go slow to avoid detection. Their weapon supply was low, and hopefully they would not have another encounter before departing. Although they had updated the council of their progress, they still needed to figure out how to contact their inside confidant.

As Tamir-Benob made his way through the brush, he sensed others ahead coming in from a separate location than the other men. These were familiar scents from the holding compound. Oddly, one was the scent of the female who injected him with some elixir. It was still confusing to him that a woman was serving in such a volatile military situation. In his world females were not warriors. Much has changed over the years.

His ability to detect different human scents was better than that of a canine. Thoughts of vengeance pleased him. He would kill them all but the woman; he would take her captive. She would serve as a hostage or a bearer of future hybrid children. It had been several hundred years since he had sired children, and they were all dead, killed by various human groups.

Dr. Mullins and Dr. Ryan entered an opening and noticed trampled grass, a sign of others walking in this area. They were a good twenty minutes from the soldiers they saw earlier and out of ear shot in a dense area.

"It'll get dark soon. Not sure if we're doing any good here. Might as well go back to the rendezvous site." Suggested Dr. Ryan.

"Yes, you're probably right. I had hoped to find more signs before now. No update from Stone, but when we get back, let's inquire if any of the others have had any sightings. I'm curious if the Indian Affairs agent has had any luck. Subject Alpha may be long gone at this point," Advised Dr. Mullins.

As Gunther and Giovanni made their way through the woods, they noticed something was following them, albeit very discreetly. They had hoped the predator had not picked up their trail. Gunther circled around behind a tree and could see the shape of the giant approaching slowly. They had overheard the small military party just ahead of them and decided the best way to lose the beast was to let the military deal with him. During the ensuing firefight they would escape. They slowed just enough to allow the giant to almost catch them and then entered the clearing with guns drawn surprising the military team.

"Everyone stand down and place your weapons on the ground." Gunther ordered.

"What is the meaning of this?" asked Mullins. "You are interfering with official US military business and need to drop your weapons and leave now."

As Mullins and Ryan contemplated their next step, Tamir-Benob stepped through an opening in the brush. He was frightening to look at, with blood streaked down his chest, signs of bullet wounds that had not yet healed on his body, and a look of malevolence on his face. He looked like a character out of a make-believe book.

The soldier providing protection for the military physicians raised his rifle to shoot, but the giant threw a spear at lightning speed that tore into the soldier's chest cavity instantly killing him. The soldier fell over dead, while the others stared in shock.

Mullins decided to act. He took a chance and spoke the secret code word to Gunther. Gunther, surprised, nodded and motioned for Mullins to join him and Giovanni.

"What are you doing, Dr. Mullins? How do you know these men? I don't understand," Dr. Ryan uttered in disbelief.

"Such naivete, Dr. Ryan. You should understand how the world works. This knowledge commands much on the black market. There is a coming apocalypse. The US military will not be able to stop the fallen and their disciples when they return to this earth. There will be thousands like this one here. When that time comes, I prefer to be part of the winning side."

"The fallen? You sound like a cult member! You can't be serious," she exclaimed.

Dr. Mullins reached over and shoved her hard in the direction of the advancing giant, who was now only a few steps away. "Take her, and we will leave you alone," Mullins said, offering Dr. Ryan to the Nephilim.

Dr. Ryan tried to stabilize herself as she fell forward.

Gunther and Giovanni raised their rifles ready to fire, but Mullins waved them down.

"No, Dr. Ryan, not a cult member, just someone well-read on the coming world events, unlike you and the others."

Tamir-Benob looked at the men warily and was momentarily confused. Mullins repeated his offer for him to take Dr. Ryan and leave them. She struggled to stand, her feet slipping in the slippery leaves laying across the trail. Tamir-Benob picked up Dr. Ryan and placed her over his shoulder while she kicked and tried to get away.

"You can't do this, Mullins. This is so wrong! Have you no conscious? How could you?" she screamed with audible terror in her voice.

The humanoid looking giant slowly backed away and moved through the brush distancing himself from the men. A momentary retreat, but he would find these men again.

Mullins turned to Gunther. "I'm the agent working with van Wilhelm."

"Yes, Dr. Mullins, we were instructed to bring you with us to our compound in Europe to continue this work."

"Excellent. Are there others on the extraction team?"

"We had several others, but they were killed by the beast. We decided to retreat and fight another day. The DNA sample is in route to Europe to your new lab, as that was the primary mission. We need to contact our local pilot before returning to Europe. He is awaiting several miles from here."

"I can help with our transport issue. We can go back a mile or so to a military checkpoint and commandeer a transport vehicle. In the confusion of this situation no one will ask who you are. We can then travel to a more remote area and meet your pickup and depart."

"That will work. We have a helicopter waiting. Although, we will need to be quick before they realize you are gone," Gunther said.

⇝⇝⤜⤜

After Tamir-Benob walked a good distance, he put a petrified Dr. Ryan down.

"If you draw others to us, I will kill you," he declared.

Shocked that he spoke English, she asked, "Why are you doing this?"

He laughed. "I will tell you later. Not the time to talk now." He picked her up and continued walking toward the distant mountain range.

# Chapter Nine

# Time to Regroup

**W**HITMAN AND HIS TEAM discovered a dead US soldier while tracking and quickly made their way to the military checkpoint. They were unable to reach Mullins but had found out a few hours ago he requested a military vehicle and was accompanied by two unknown men. That was strange, but Whitman did not have time to investigate now. It was getting dark, and unfortunately, they had to assume that their quarry was heading toward the mountains. Tracks led around the military checkpoint, showing a deliberate avoidance. Whitman decided at this point it was best to get some rest and meet his men at this location early in the morning.

After being treated by the military medic Stone had managed a few hours' sleep and was up early on the phone the next morning with General Briggs.

The General was barking questions. "Where are Mullins and Ryan? They're not answering their phones, and no one has seen them since yesterday."

"They left yesterday afternoon toward Subject Alpha's last known location. The security agent with them was found dead. Dr. Ryan is missing, and Dr. Mullins was last seen at a checkpoint with two unknown men. The car he left in has not been found. He either left under duress or is AWOL."

"Makes little sense about Mullins. He's a career military man and led numerous projects. This kind of thing just does not happen. Try and find Ryan, but our priority is Subject Alpha. We'll need to work with Indian Affairs. Our projection based on his last coordinates puts him close to the Crow Reservation and the mountains nearby. That's a big reservation, and there a lot of places to hide, even for something this large."

"More troops are arriving within the hour General, and we will be out searching as soon as possible."

"Keep me posted of any progress."

Whitman had gone home for a few hours of sleep and then returned to the tribal headquarters office for a meeting with his team and several tribe members. He had plotted out a map of possible directions the beast could be heading and addressed the group in the early morning.

"The few of us who interacted with him would estimate his height to be at least ten-to-eleven feet and his weight at over a thousand pounds. We have confirmed he has killed several soldiers over the last two days. We confronted him in Coup State Park. During the encounter I shot him twice in the chest with a Remington 870, and he walked away with minimal injuries. Security Chief Stone, who was providing support for the military compound, also shot him center mass prior to my encounter. Subject Alpha seems to have a regenerative capability that allows him to recover from wounds that would kill a normal man. He is now most likely heading toward the Pryor Mountains, traveling at about twice the speed of a normal Crow warrior," recapped Ironhorse.

Mighty Eagle chimed in. "This is as bad as we have feared, Ironhorse. Our people are in grave danger. This is a repeat of the early legends from hundreds of years ago."

"We will find him and stop him. We have no other choice," Ironhorse forcefully stated who then quickly assigned roles.

A team of men would go with him to track the giant. Several others would go ahead of his group in pairs to track and rule out where the giant was not heading, with instructions not to engage. Tribesman who would not evacuate were warned to stay in hiding and would serve as extra eyes if the subject showed up. They also called in an IA helicopter patrol to help with an aerial search.

"Based on where we last spotted him yesterday, a logical direction from topography and nearest mountains would be

West Pryor Mountain. There are several caves and underground tunnels he could hide out in. If he manages to reach one of those, especially one of the ice caverns, he will be extremely difficult to extract without many deaths. We need to find him soon."

As the team left for their assignments, Mighty Eagle pulled Whitman aside. "Ironhorse, for your battle I have a few tribal talismans. These will help protect you. The first is an ancient tomahawk, which has been refitted with steel and a blade sharpened with a razor edge. It will cut through the hardest material. Also, a tribal amulet, which will protect you in battle. It was worn by our first chief when our people settled here. He wore it into battle with the earlier red-haired giants who attacked our people many years ago. It was blessed by our spiritual leaders and is a sacred amulet of protection."

"Thank you, Mighty Eagle. I will wear it proudly. I'm bringing several high-powered rifles and plan to take our opponent by surprise and stealth. We may not have the firepower to stop him, but we will give it everything we have."

Whitman quickly departed and took his team toward the mountains. They packed weapons, food, and maps, although most of them knew the land well enough to navigate without one. Horses would be waiting for them at the forest line, and the trackers were already out searching.

⋙⋙ ⋘⋘

Tamir-Benob was making fast time, approaching the base of the mountain before sunrise. Dr. Ryan had tried multiple times to escape but was not able to get away. Each time he threatened her with physical harm.

He spotted a small home in a clearing as they made their way through the forest. He needed nourishment but had to keep the woman close. There was cattle and livestock near the house. If anyone lived there, he would kill them to prevent discovery. As he stopped running, he dropped Dr. Ryan to the ground. She landed hard, her back hurting from being carried.

"What are you doing? Let me go you monster!" Dr. Ryan yelled. Her fear intensified the further they traveled. Her chances for escape were running out.

Tamir-Benob just stared at her and then grabbed the goat nearby. He sunk his razor-sharp teeth into the helpless animal and satisfied his hunger. Dr. Ryan looked away in disgust. The smell of blood and the sound of bone crunching overwhelmed her senses.

"Meat?"

"No, I would rather go hungry than accept anything from you."

The giant didn't seem to need sleep, but she would soon tire out. The house was empty, so she begged for a break. After resting for only about a half hour, the giant snatched her up aggressively and continued their trek onward. She could see the peak of the mountains. They had probably covered over twenty miles during the night. At this rate it would be difficult for anyone to find them. She was still confused about why Dr. Mullins had given her to Subject Alpha. They were at a higher elevation, and it was getting colder. Fortunately, it was still early fall, and the winter snow had not arrived. She closed her eyes and tried to think of how she could fight this behemoth. Perhaps since Subject Alpha was highly intelligent, she could appeal to him on an intellectual level when they stopped to rest again. There must be a way to reason with him.

Mullins and his benefactors had ditched their military vehicle awhile back. They decided to take a pre-arranged car out of the vicinity rather than draw attention with air transport. Time was of the essence, as the military would be looking for Mullins once his recent disappearance was discovered. A charter jet was arranged near Bismarck, North Dakota, at a private landing field. This would give them enough separation to use air transport. After disposing of anything that could link them to the military, the group had driven through the night to reach the airport.

Mullins knew he had a different life ahead and was looking forward to starting his next chapter. He could only imagine what had happened to Dr. Ryan. There was no malice intended for her, but there was little recourse in the situation, and she had to be sacrificed. She was probably dead by now. Hopefully, her death was quick.

The group's mission was most important for him, as his studies with various religious texts had convinced him of man's future. He had an opportunity now to shape the destiny of the world, and he wouldn't miss his chance to be part of something so impactful. The Council of Five's reach was unknown to him, and he only knew the small pieces that van Wilhelm had shared. Man in its current state of evolution was not ready for the change coming, but they would get there or be conquered. He smiled in anticipation as they continued their drive.

Whitman and his team started in the direction Subject Alpha had recently traveled. He spoke with the officer in charge at the military facility. The post was short staffed, and the soldiers arriving were bolstering security and the holding cell before working to maintain a perimeter while Whitman's team tracked the escaped subject. Whitman would call in the military once his team had located Subject Alpha. Stone showed up at the rendezvous spot heavily armed and wanted to participate in the hunt.

"Do you think you can handle this, Stone?"

"Of course, I'm up for it, and I need to do this."

"Ok, your call. But we aren't slowing down for you."

One more highly trained soldier could only be helpful, Whitman thought before addressing his team. "Most likely we're a good six hours or so behind when these tracks were made. He can travel land at least twice as fast as a normal man, so he's several miles ahead of us right now. Let's use our horses to make up distance. Realistically we're going to have to follow him into the mountains and caves. Mighty Eagle has several warriors ready as reinforcements if needed. We leave in five minutes, so take care of any last items."

⟫⟫ ⟪⟪

General Briggs was frustrated with the entire situation. He could not figure out how Subject Alpha escaped and what happened to Dr. Mullins and Dr. Ryan. Drones had been authorized to help in the search, and homeland security had been put on alert for the missing physicians. Stone was allowed to go in the field to help in the search, and their investigative team was looking hard for Dr. Mullins. His vehicle was found outside of Billings Montana, at least thirty miles away from the previous military checkpoint. Mullins must have had others help on this, and he was most likely long gone. He would be considered a security risk given his knowledge of top-secret research programs.

The US president and the governor of Montana had been updated, and the governor was preparing to declare a statewide emergency. Indian Affairs would hold priority on the reservation, but the governor would dictate next steps outside reservation land. The president had refrained from taking more drastic action so far, but he may have to step in if the situation deteriorated any further.

"This is Briggs. Let's convene the group tonight for an update," the general said to an unknown voice on the other end of the line.

"Understood, General. The others have several questions and want to know how the current events impact next steps. I will arrange the meeting at the normal location."

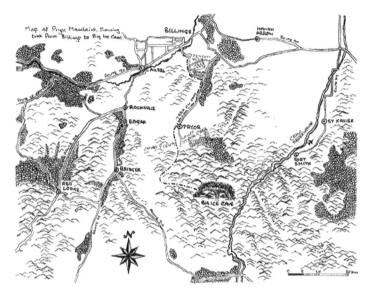

*Escape From Secret Military Base Near Pryor Mountain*

# Chapter Ten
# Base of West Pryor Mountains

TAMIR-BENOB WAS RUNNING ON the wooded trail and stopped to rest near a stream shadowed by large trees. The area was remote and far away from the hands of man. He put the woman down and noticed two animals moving nearby, a small one and a much larger one. They looked like the bears from his adopted home, but these had brown fur and humped shoulders. Their ears were short, and the larger one had long claws. Most likely this was a baby with a parent, and the larger bear growled and hunched up in an attack stance.

"A grizzly bear!" Dr. Ryan shouted, looking on in horror as the larger one was nearly eight feet tall and weighed several hundred pounds. This was the most dangerous predator in the forest. She had no good choices—be taken away by Subject Alpha or be mauled to death by a grizzly. She really wished she had a gun.

Tamir-Benob beat his chest like a gladiator issuing a challenge. The mother bear roared back at the giant, clawing the giant back and leaving a blood mark on his chest.

Ryan didn't know whether to try to help her attacker or the bear.

The bear continued to attack in a frenzy trying to maul and bite its red-haired opponent. Tamir-Benob stood up, caught the bear, and held it in place so that he was just out of reach of the bear's snapping jaws. He took several hits from its razor-sharp claws, which drew blood and left stinging wounds. The giant threw the bear down hard against a tree. Howling in pain, the animal jumped up and attacked again with fury in her eyes.

Tamir-Benob picked up a nearby tree branch and used it as a club to hit the raging animal in the head, knocking it back dazed. As he walked over to finish his opponent off, the grizzly swung wildly and caught Tamir-Benob in the leg with a claw, pulling off a chunk of flesh. The giant howled in pain and limped back. He then jumped on the bear and put the creature in a choke hold.

The grizzly thrashed around wildly trying to break free from the death grip. It viciously bit at Tamir-Benob's arms, drawing more blood. They rolled on the ground, two titans battling, their growls shattering the silence in the forest.

Ryan looked on in horror but was too mesmerized by the spectacle to intervene. Finally, the bear stopped moving, its life taken with a broken neck.

The behemoth of a man slowly pushed the bear off him and stood up victorious with a wild rage in his eyes. He was terrifying to look at, a titan with no equals. He slowly stepped into the nearby stream to wash the blood off him. Exiting the water like a demigod, he shook his hair like a wild animal. Multiple cuts and contusions and a gaping wound remained in his leg.

He pointed to his leg and said, "You're a healer. Fix my leg, woman."

"How did you learn our language?"

"Take care of leg now, talk later," Tamir-Benob ordered her with irritation.

"Ok, ok. I'll fix it now." She approached the giant cautiously, as the baby grizzly scampered away. Ryan took a gauze and some tape out of the medical kit she had managed to hold on to. She held it up and pointed to Tamir-Benob's wound to let him know she would bandage the bloody area. As she approached, she felt so diminutive compared to him. She sensed he was watching her and was fearful he might decide to kill her instead. The injury was already beginning to heal. The regenerative capabilities were incredible. There was no explanation for this. After taping up the wound the best she could, he told her to sit.

"I will gather food and build a small fire. If you try to leave, I will know and track you down. Do not anger me if you want to live. Stay here and I will be back shortly."

'What choice do I have?"

"None."

The giant walked away into the forest, and Ryan contemplated whether to run or stay. She knew his heightened senses could track her, and he would easily overtake her. She was too far in the wild to make it back, so it would probably be better to wait on a different opportunity to escape. She hopelessly looked over at the dead bear and contemplated her next step.

⤜⤜⤜ ⤛⤛⤛

Whitman's team had traveled rapidly for about two hours on horseback to try and make up ground. They had stopped only briefly to rest the horses. His scouts had confirmed their direction was accurate. They were running close to Pryor Creek. The military had nothing new to report.

One of his trackers had found human tracks intermingled with the giant's traveling through the forest. They were intermittent and seemed only to appear when the giant stopped to rest. Given their size and contour, the tracks were most likely female. This meant someone else was at risk and they would have to alter their approach to the giant. Whitman alerted Stone and the others.

"Given the disappearance of Dr. Ryan and the dead soldier in the meadow, it's probable that Subject Alpha has Dr. Ryan with him." Whitman stating what the others were thinking.

"Is there any reason to believe she's still alive?" asked Stone.

"Yes, I believe so based on our tracker's observation. She has been missing since interacting with him in the state park

121

yesterday. Not sure of his rationale for taking her. We do not have a good read on how this thing thinks or if it thinks at all."

"When we woke Subject Alpha, Dr. Ryan had some contentious conversation with him. He told us he would take our women. He gave her especially hateful looks. I'm surprised he didn't kill her when he saw her," Stone said. "The creature is very smart, and he was studying us, biding his time to make his move."

"That's helpful. The creature has always been an alpha predator, something from a long-ago age. Perhaps he saw her defiance as a strength. That could create some degree of respect, although I'm not sure if that would keep her alive. Hopefully he doesn't have other nefarious ideas," Whitman stated.

Before taking off with his team, Whitman was reminded of his recent dreams where he was fighting a large red-haired man in the caves. He was losing the battle, but something changed the tide. Mighty Eagle had counseled him that it would make sense when the time was right, as that was the way of the Great Spirit. He wished the Great Spirit would share insight with him right now.

Miles away from everything happening in the forest, Gunther boarded the private plane parked south of Bismarck. The pilot fired up the engine of the Gulfstream G650ER as soon as the passengers were on board. They would fly through the night to land near Maine at another airport and change planes. This was a charter flight, and it would be good to get on their European-bound flight. Mullins had changed his clothes, added a wig with glasses, and was given a fake German passport. As far as American customs officials were concerned, they were just three businessmen returning to Europe from a successful trip. The authorities would not think to look for Mullins along the New England coast, especially sporting a different appearance. They discarded their weapons and settled back for a hot meal and a little sleep before arriving to the East Coast.

## Chapter Eleven
# In the Depths of the Forest

**T**AMIR-BENOB HAD GATHERED SEVERAL roots and berries in his hunt. He had also killed a deer—fresh venison was always tasty. Unlike his children over the years, the Elioud, who preferred to consume the blood and meat from their kills uncooked, he preferred to cook his meat when possible. Living in caves in the far away land did not allow that often. That existence seemed liked punishment. In his youth he had been part of an army, took what he wanted, and lived like a king. The Philistine people treated him like a god.

That had changed with the Israeli son of YHVH. Those were terrible memories, and he would not be hunted like that again. It was time for his kind to reassert dominance over man.

His senses told him the female was still nearby. *Good*. He did not want to have to pursue her. The female showed courage, but she still needed to learn her role. He walked into the clearing where she was standing and threw his kill on the ground.

"Wash the roots and berries. I will prepare a fire and cook the meat. You must eat to keep strength before we continue." He was confident they had time given the speed he had traversed through the forest. But he didn't want to take too long, lest the warriors catch them.

"You expect me to eat wild roots? And an animal you killed?"

"Yes, it will provide nourishment. The roots and berries are safe for you to eat. Now prepare. We have little time."

Ryan begrudgingly did her best to make a salad out of the leaves, berries, and roots available. In a different setting, this might even be considered rustic or farm-to-table.

Tamir-Benob skinned the deer with a knife he had been carrying and constructed a makeshift tepee using tree limbs to roast meat from the animal. He used a couple of pumice and quartz rocks he'd picked up near the stream to create a spark and start a fire. After he cooked the venison for some time, he pulled off the best steak and offered it to Dr. Ryan.

"Here, eat this with the plants," he said, shoving the steak toward her.

Ryan thought the meat smelled good but refused to admit it to her captor. She didn't want to eat, but it had been a day since she had any nourishment, and she was famished. She took the meat reluctantly and ate it. Maybe it was her starvation talking, but she was surprised at how good it tasted. She munched on the plants for their additional needed nutrients.

Tamir-Benob sat and ate the remainder of the venison, followed by the berries. It was filling, and it had been close to a week's time since he'd had a cooked meal. After dinner they drank water from the stream and rested.

Ryan decided to take a chance and to try to speak to the beast now. "I helped prepare the meal. You said we could speak, and I have questions for you."

"We have a little time, so I will answer a few questions now."

"Ok. Who are you and where do you come from?"

"I will not answer that fully, as my story takes too long to tell, but I come from along ago land and from a since destroyed race. We were warriors and rulers of this world. My people were a product of the mighty spirit men, fallen sons and holy messengers of the Hebrew God. I am one of the few remaining. That is all I will say for now. Your people pursue the last of my kind. If they catch us, it will be a big mistake on their part. We must leave now. Ask no more of me."

Using a hollow looking rock, Tamir-Benob carried over some water and doused the fire and used his feet to stamp out the remaining embers.

Ryan had hoped for a breakthrough, but his answers were matter of fact, devoid of emotion. "I can walk," offered Ryan, hoping to slow him down.

"No, too slow." With that he picked her up like a feather, threw her over his sweaty shoulder, and took off in a jog toward the mountains nearby.

The two Crow scouts had stayed down wind. The giant was not trying to hide his tracks, so they were able to follow his steps and slowly catch up to him. They were exhausted at this pace, as nothing this large in the wild could move this fast. A few miles down wind they picked up the faintest scent of smoke. This deep in the forest, it would be rare for a fire to be built. Given that their fellow tribesmen were warned by IA to stay away from this part of the reservation, the fire was most likely from the quarry they were tracking. The scouts stopped to give Whitman an update of their findings and get instructions for next steps.

Whitman and his team were about five miles behind the location of their recent scout reporting. He would hold off on sending a helicopter to avoid endangering Dr. Ryan. His team could travel on horseback another few miles before going on foot. The location of the giant was only a few miles from the base of the mountain and where the caves started. They had to make up ground before the mountains and cave system. Some of the caves connected, and if the giant and his hostage made it there, it would be near impossible to track them down or approach in stealth. As a backup plan, they would have the chopper waiting to intervene before they entered any of the caves.

Whitman encouraged the team to move faster, although they were exhausted from the pace.

He tried to provide encouragement. "Ramos and Running Wolf may have a lead on the giant. They're a few miles downwind but have found tracks and smoke from a fire deep in the forest. The other trackers will convene to help out."

Stone asked, "How far away are we? Is there a short cut to reach them?"

"We're about six or seven miles behind. There's a ranch about halfway where we should be able to pick up fresh horses. We can ask Mighty Eagle and his group to slow them down or at least better pinpoint their location. Let's double-time it now, and I will let the others know of our plan."

With a grim determination, the men picked up their pace through the rough terrain.

Mighty Eagle received Ironhorse's call and quickly gathered another group of Crow tribesman and other IA officers at the reservation headquarters. Based on their trackers, the giant had passed through West Pryor Mountain and was moving in parallel to Pryor Creek toward Big Pryor Mountain and ice caves. There were several other small caves along the way, and it would be getting dark soon, which complicated things.

Mighty Eagle brought along dynamite and high temperature burn logs in the event they could trap the giant in one of the caves.

⋙ ⋘

Darkness was fast approaching, and several stars were visible to guide the way. Tamir-Benob did not recognize the star alignment, but a small cave was several meters ahead. They would use it for shelter for the night. The cave was somewhat hidden, on a hill and would provide adequate cover. If others approached, he would be able to see them coming. The warriors were most likely following him now. The one with black hair who shot him with the firestick a day ago most likely would lead them. He welcomed the future battle, but he needed to get further away, more isolated, which would favor him. Isolation would make it easier to kill them one by one.

"We will stop here, in the cave. Rest for the night," he said.

"In the cave? Near other animals? How do we keep warm?" Dr. Ryan asked, agitated by the suggestion of less than comfortable sleeping arrangements.

"I will make sure there are no animals. No need for warmth. We will sleep on the ground."

"What about a fire?"

"Fire will give away our location. No fire."

Ryan was not happy about the lack of a fire. She'd had little sleep over the past two days, and the idea of sleeping on a dark, musty cave floor with snakes and spiders was not appealing. Maybe she could use nearby leaves and pine needles for a cushion or pillow? As they entered the cave, she heard the pitter-patter of feet back in the cave. Subject Alpha ran and stomped on the furry animal. It sounded disgusting. He came back and pushed some rocks aside. Using several large leaves, he made a makeshift bed for her.

"You sleep here," he grunted. "I will sleep sitting up. No bears will enter cave. Rest now."

Ryan placed her military jacket on the ground for use as a blanket and tried to get comfortable. It would be a long night. She decided to try one more time to speak with him. The giant had settled down with his head resting against a rock. His eyes were already shut. Even when he was resting, she could tell his senses were on high alert.

"I have more questions, and you were going to answer them later. Will you finally speak to me?"

The giant opened his eyes and gave her a piercing glance. "Ok, a few questions. Then you must sleep. Tomorrow will be a long day. They are getting closer."

Ryan thought for a moment, as this might be her only chance to speak with him, especially with the military most likely in hot pursuit. "Is the parchment in the cave we found yours?"

In a slow measured tone, the hybrid man spoke. "The parchment your people stole is mine. It contains a record of my life deeds, as those before me have recorded their deeds. I am what the prophet Moses called a Nephilim, half man and half spirit. My father was the second born of a nameless, powerful fallen spirit son of the Creator from after the time of the great flood. My father was a giant and my mother a powerful witch. Most of your people do not believe in the existence of my kind."

"I thought Nephilim were mythical. What do you know of the fallen spirit sons of the Creator?" she asked him.

"They were fallen angels of the most high, who shared knowledge instead of just watching and decided to mate with humankind. From our legends, this happened after the great flood waters that followed the time of the great shipbuilder. None of our elders from that time were alive during my youth. I was a grandson of a fallen, and my children were great grandchildren of these mighty beings."

"Have you met any of these fallen spirit sons?"

"I was visited by a chief amongst the spirit sons in my cave many moons ago. Their power is great, with an appearance that is grotesque and fearful compared to man. He told me that there were others of my kind still living and that one day we would make war on your kind and retake the lands. He counseled patience and that other fallen spirit sons would return as a powerful army, led by the mighty heylel, the light-bearer, the one who was cast from the heavens in the beginning. I have not seen any more fallen spirit sons since then. Although my father had many interactions with his father."

"Heylel? Is that Lucifer?"

"He has numerous names, and Lucifer has been used. He was one of the first for the Creator, and he is destined to rule this realm. Many are waiting on his return."

"Some would disagree with that. Tell me, how old exactly are you, and when were you born?"

"Many years ago, before the time of David. I was a young warrior when he became king."

"That was over three thousand years ago?" she questioned.

"Yes, I am older than most of my kind. My lineage probably explains that. Most of my brothers lived less than five hundred mortal years, but I am different. My lineage is from a very powerful fallen."

"And did you witness Goliath and David battle?"

"Yes, David was the favored of the Hebrew God. In those days, the Creator's hand was more evident in man's daily workings. I see his hand and his messengers less today, as man ignores him. David would not have stunned Goliath with his rocks without divine help. The boy was a good servant, if you prefer to spend your days praying, and making sacrifices."

"And Goliath?"

"Goliath was a famous Rapha. He and my father were brothers. Born from the same fallen son of the Creator. They trained me to fight. Both were killed by David and his servant. They would have lived thousands of years with their progeny. I killed many of his soldiers, but his army was too powerful," he said passionately.

"Is that how you ended up in your current home?"

"I have lived in several locations and witnessed many things. Too many phenomenal events to describe to you." He took a small pause and then continued, "When I arrived years ago to the land you call Afghanistan, the Mongols were there, and the kin of the Great Khan challenged my dominance. The rivers turned red before their final defeat. I grew tired of man's interference and moved to the caves. The caves are desolate, and mainly hunters and travelers approach those areas. The few that bothered me did not again."

"Since you say you lived so long and are a mighty warrior, what about other world rulers? Did you interact with them?"

"The battles were too numerous to count, the blood too deep to measure. The other names your history might recognize whom my kind has warred with include Alexander, Julius Caesar, and Attila the Hun."

"Why do you hate man so much? What is the point?"

"Man is like a child that does not learn and doesn't belong. Your kind sees little of how things really exist. You think in one dimension, but there is a spiritual realm that is so much more important. Many of my deceased kind reside there, and it is not an unknown afterlife. Even with all this ignorance, the Creator values you more than my kind and as much as the spirit men. And you ask why I hate such a weak species?"

"Tell me more about the spiritual realm," Dr. Ryan asked, truly curious about what he might say.

"The spiritual realm is a place my kind go after physical death, but without mortal body. Not the same as where man's spirits go, but near enough to this world to observe and occasionally interact. They are biding time to make their way back to the world. One day when the door opens, they will return."

"What will open the door for them?"

"Several things must happen. I have been told that once man forsakes the teachings of the Creator, the fallen may return in physical form. It will be subtle at first. Man will not notice before it is too late. Look around, the world is changing, and in many places, there is no faith in the Creator. During that time my kind, the children of the fallen, will multiply. Man in its foolishness will also allow more of my kind to return from the spiritual realm, either through open invitation to the soul, or through man's efforts to recreate more of my kind artificially."

"I'm not sure if I believe you, but I do have one last question about your past. Did you interact with the Christian Messiah, Jesus Christ?"

"Do you mean Yeshua from Nazareth, Son of the Creator?"

"Yes, the Creator's holy son."

"I avoided the Nazarene and his disciples. He was the Son of the Highest. The angels of the Hebrew God would have destroyed me if I had approached him, I am convinced."

"Angels?"

"Yes, the angels of the Hebrew God. They exist in this world, but man is oblivious to them. I have seen them, and more than once they stayed my hand from destruction."

"Really, as in bright light, wings...?"

"No, they do not display wings, they appeared as mortal men, but had unstoppable strength and extrasensory abilities."

Ryan still remained skeptical of his tales.

"What about now, what do you expect to happen, and why did you take me?"

"I was taken from my land by force, by soldiers without my permission. They will die for that. Then I will look for others like me."

"The soldiers coming are strong and powerful. There are many."

"I have killed many already. After tonight we will continue to move further into the caves. I will use you as a shield against the men, or possibly as a mother for my children."

Ryan couldn't believe what she had just heard. *Mother for his children?* She was not going to allow that to happen. For now, she would bide her time, and not show her shock. "Do you have many children?"

"All my children are dead. They were hunted because they could not control their hungers and created conflict with man. But I will make more. This time I will control them better." He turned, told her he would speak no more and to go to sleep.

Ryan sat for a long time until she heard the giant sleeping. Should she use a rock to crush his skull? Should she sneak out and run away? Neither seemed likely to succeed. Perhaps she could leverage an opportunity when the others arrived. She knew Whitman and the others would come, but it was a matter of when. Hopefully the others would be there soon, time was running short.

# Chapter Twelve

# Another Dangerous Encounter

**G**EORGE RAMOS AND RUNNING **Wolf were close to** their quarry. Both were expert woodsmen and young warriors of the Crow tribe. They quickly volunteered to help Ironhorse. They started well before sunlight to make up time. On their last stop they had updated Whitman as to their location. A dead grizzly bear less than a day old was found. The way the grizzly was killed was a sure sign of the giant—something super strong, not typical for the wild had invaded the forest. They would have to be extra cautious in their approach. Signs of Dr. Ryan were also present. They would catch up with them soon.

⊱⊱⊱ ⊰⊰⊰

Tamir-Benob woke early and noted the woman asleep. His instincts told him others were close. His half-angelic heritage had given him intensely honed senses of hearing and smell to detect others from miles away.

The trackers were quietly making their way toward them. He had not smelled the scent of these warriors before. Both were unknown to him. He would surprise the newcomers before they arrived. His heart rate picked up. Although he was large in size, he made little sound as he exited the cave under the cover of darkness. An owl watched from his safe perch high in a tree as the giant melted into the forest. Clouds blocked out most of the moonlight.

⊱⊱⊱ ⊰⊰⊰

The sun had not yet risen in the part of the forest where Whitman had spent the night. He'd only managed a few hours of restless sleep. Exhaustion was quickly over taking the men. The others worked quietly to be prepared for departure on a moment's notice, taking advantage of precious minutes to hydrate and gulp caffeine for a bolt of energy.

Stone pulled Whitman aside. "Any news from the trackers?"

"They're close to the creature. A dead grizzly carcass was found at his rest spot, probably killed yesterday, so we have a chance to catch him today."

"He has some type of heightened senses, so if they get too close, he'll know," Stone warned.

"Not surprising but doesn't change anything for us. Before long he'll be too far up in the mountains to catch. My goal is to get close enough and find a way to engage him. On our route we'll pick up some horses and a few more reinforcements."

"I need to update General Briggs. Given the terrain and being that we're on the Crow Reservation, he most likely will want you to handle the initial encounter. Depending on the outcome, he'll assess whether to send in troops and air support. We can ask for a helicopter extraction if needed," offered Stone.

Whitman felt the heavy burden of what was to come. Most likely many of the men with him would die and never return home. A sobering thought. He wished he could call this off and send them home. But he knew the death toll would only increase without help from his people. The last of his men picked up their packs and weapons and waited on his order to move out, stoically anticipating the battle with Subject Alpha later that day.

The two warriors looked around cautiously, as the forest had grown silent. Ramos signaled Running Wolf to move slowly. Something did not feel right. They were within a mile or so from their target based on the trail signs. Ramos tightened his grip on his knife a little harder in anticipation. Sweat dripped slowly down his cheek as he strained to hear the slightest noise or any unnatural movement.

Tamir-Benob had caught up with the two Crow trackers making their way toward the cave he and the woman had spent the night in. He'd stayed downwind, so they were unaware of his stealthy approach. He watched them move forward cautiously with a stone-cold look in their eyes.

He studied the men. They were from the same tribe as the warrior who shot him. These were worthy opponents, experts of the forest, something he rarely saw. He did not detect anyone else close by, so he would only be dealing with these two men. Approaching quietly downwind from their rear would give him the element of surprise. The two were moving slowly toward a large stack of rocks, which would limit their escape route.

The giant swooped out of a clearing from behind like a storm, holding a spear he had made the previous night. There was no emotion, just focus on confronting them. Both tribesmen heard his approach and turned together to face him. They knew their only option was to fight to survive.

Running Wolf reacted instantly and threw his tomahawk at the charging giant as he rushed forward, hitting him in the shoulder. The quick move and the resulting pain threw the giant off balance. He pulled the weapon out of his shoulder and tossed it aside as blood ran down his torso. Both warriors stood their ground.

"First blood. Excellent, I would expect nothing less," Tamir-Benob said, turning to look directly at the determined Crow warriors.

"You are just as evil as our elders warned us about," Running Wolf challenged, trying to distract the beast.

"So, my kind has been here before?"

Ramos snapped up his rifle and fired three shots, hitting the giant in the chest. More blood streamed down, and an angry Tamir-Benob threw his spear with such ferocity that he impaled Running Wolf to a nearby tree.

"You killed him you animal!" Ramos shouted before throwing his knife blade at the Nephilim's head. Unfortunately for Ramos, the giant's big hand reached up and caught the knife.

Tamir-Benob laughed at the slash the blade left in his palm. He tossed the knife on the ground and stepped forward. "Valliant effort, warrior, but I will not be taken that easily."

The Crow warrior pulled his pistol and fired multiple shots at the behemoth lumbering toward him. A normal individual would be dead. Ramos stood determined to hold his ground as he waited for the beast's next attack.

Tamir-Benob stepped forward again and grabbed the young warrior. He held him close. "Time for this to end."

The giant's breath was rancid, his eyes orange-black and piercing. Ramos head-butted the giant, breaking his nose, and eliciting a roar in pain. Ramos was dropped to the ground and caught with a backhand across the face. He grimaced at the broken bones, but struggled to get up, trying to block out the pain.

Tamir-Benob kicked hard, knocking Ramos against a tree with a force that rendered the warrior unconscious. Unsure if the man was dead, Tamir-Benob decided to go back to the cave for the woman and move further into the wilderness.

⇒⇒⇒ ⇐⇐⇐

Mighty Eagle was waiting for Whitman at their meeting spot with fresh horses and supplies. Reinforcements were joining the hunt. They rode together at a face pace.

"I have this overwhelming premonition of bloodshed and death, like the dreams we spoke about," Ironhorse confided in his friend.

"Unfortunately, bloodshed and death are inevitable in this life. Like our ancestors, we must face down this evil, together as brothers," Mighty Eagle responded.

"Many of these brave warriors won't return to their family. My heart wants to send them home, but we will need them all to succeed."

"They would never turn back; our people are proud. Lead them and believe in yourself. You are the only one who can lead us."

"What do the spirits say?"

"The spirits will give you strength. Dreams are how they communicate, and they wouldn't enter yours unless they wanted you to succeed. The giant draws on powers from the spirit realm and his magic is great. But even though he is part spirit, he is still mortal. If you can knock him unconscious you can take his head, or if we trap him in the cave a strong fire will burn or suffocate him. He most likely can die," Mighty Eagle continued. "We do not want the US military to capture him, as they will only make our challenge greater. Can you imagine an army of soldiers going rogue with these capabilities? That would only end in more death."

"Your words hold true. But I fear our ability to overcome his strength. When you see him, you'll be shocked at how powerful and unnatural he appears," Whitman said, with doubt creeping up in his voice.

"I have some special tricks lined up when we do encounter him," Mighty Eagle said as a sly smile spread across his face.

Stone had listened quietly to the conversation between the Crow leaders. He felt an obligation to the military to capture the creature but understood how dangerous it would be if the government got its hands on this thing. He worried about the possibility of DNA manipulation and the implications of those kinds of experiments. Although he recalled Mullins sending DNA out for study, he was unsure if that had actually happened. More worrisome was whether Mullins sent the sample to some rogue government. A lot for him to contemplate. He was not a religious person, but this shed a new light on the existence of a supernatural world with other creatures more powerful than man. Was organized religion correct in their thinking?

As they made their way along the trail, Whitman decided to activate the IA helicopter team to help in the search. He wanted his team nearby before the military sent their own choppers in. The last thing he needed was a full-scale military incursion on tribal land.

General Briggs had finally spoken to Stone and decided to send more troops toward the reservation. He planned to wait until Whitman and his team identified the location of Subject Alpha and then send an extraction team in. Helicopters had been sent to the military facility with additional troops armed with heavy-duty tranquilizers. The president had given the ok, and the governor was kept out of the process. There would be backlash, but it was time to end this.

Tamir-Benob made his way back to the cave where Ryan still slept. He had grabbed berries and roots along the way. The woman would need nutrition and water for the trip ahead.

Dr. Ryan awoke with a start at the sound of Tamir-Benob's heavy steps echoing off the walls. Sleeping on the cold damp floor had only added to her agitation. "Where have you been? You're covered in blood. Don't tell me you confronted more soldiers."

"Others have followed. They fought bravely but are no more."

"You didn't have to kill them." She felt sick at the thought of more innocent people dying.

"They attacked me with weapons, which was a mistake. Others will follow, so it is time to leave. Here is food, and you should drink water from the stream before we leave."

Ryan decided it would be futile to fight with the beast. She would continue to look for an opportunity for escape. The venison from yesterday had given her some strength, at least enough to be levelheaded for the day.

They walked to the creek to hydrate. The land itself was beautiful. Lots of green foliage and various kinds of trees, small and tall, surrounded them. Untouched by man's hand, the rushing sound of the clear, cold water was loud, but peaceful.

Even as the giant bent over to consume the water, he kept one eye watching outward. He was more like an animal than man. He never let his guard down.

Ryan tied her hair into a ponytail with a makeshift vine and ducked her head in the water. It felt good to wash her face and take a long drink. The forest had gone quiet, as if in deference to its new king. Slowly they began to hear the flap of wings. The sound grew as they prepared to depart. Finally, a beautiful bird with brown wings came into their view. Ryan estimated that its wingspan was close to seven feet.

"What kind of bird is that?" Tamir-Benob asked.

"A bald eagle. The symbol of our great nation," Ryan replied.

"Is this the land of the great eagle then?"

"Yes, our people have a rich history, and this noble creature represents those experiences and that belief. Why do you care?" Ryan asked sarcastically.

Ignoring her tone, the beast replied. "Several of my kinsman went to the land of the great eagle many years ago. Maybe there are still more of my kind in this land."

"I've never heard of others of your kind being in our land, but if they came here hundreds or even thousands of years ago, I assume it's possible. There is no way they could stay hidden now."

"During a visit by a fallen spirit son, I was told that my brothers had been sent to the land of the great eagle. That it was a vast land and the next great empire. He was knowledgeable about these things. Although my kind's presence started here over a thousand years ago."

"If they were here now, our military would have found them. That's not the case, so it looks like you are the only one of your kind here. You have little chance to win a fight by yourself."

"That will change. More of my people are foretold to return and rule this world."

"Man would never allow that; they are too greedy and wouldn't share power with the likes of your kind. Besides, our weapons are too powerful."

"Man relies too much on weapons and is too arrogant. That will be their downfall. When the fallen return, none of your weapons will work. We will decimate your armies, destroy your infrastructure, and kill those who will not submit to servitude."

"Our kind would never acquiesce to beasts such as you." A defiant Ryan said.

"You would be surprised at what man will do. When I was a young warrior in Gath, less than thirty of my kind ruled a city of thousands. We killed many in the beginning, and they could not stop us. My children were bloodthirsty, even drinking the blood of their victims. Over time the Nephilim brotherhood ruled the army, their king bowed to our demands, and eventually the people treated us like gods. The scribes don't report how many deaths the Philistines had before giving into our demands. Your people will do that same."

"Yes, but one great warrior of God led an army to defeat your people. It can be done again. You will not have the numbers to accomplish a takeover. There are billions of people on the planet now. It's not manageable."

"You underestimate what is waiting for your people. There are many thousands of my kind waiting in spirit form, to enter this realm. When others like me return, the fallen will also come back, and we will create more children of the Rapha. It will take several years, and much blood shed, but we will do it again, as before the great flood waters."

"What do you mean by spirits inhabiting bodies? You said this before."

"How ignorant that you do not understand the teachings of the Hebrew God? The Creator saved mankind from my people, but you still persist in disbelief. Even I heard about the Nazarene commanding spirits of my kind into swine and off the cliff into the sea. This happened during my lifetime. That was a true demonstration of power. If man is not smart enough to read the holy writings and take heed, they deserve to be conquered.

"To answer your naïve question, the spirit of my kind remain here disembodied, cursed from their mortal death, being neither truly mortal nor immortal, something in between. In the future, they will return and inhabit the bodies of others. Do you not hear their screams in the night or see how some men are influenced to do evil? My kind can return to replicated mortal bodies without souls, or from other susceptible hosts who ask them in."

"That's not possible. You're inferring possession. The human body and mind do not allow that kind of inhabitation," Ryan said, with an undertone of defiance.

"Just like it is not possible for someone of my kind to walk the earth or to defeat hundreds of your best warriors. It is foretold that when evil increases on earth, the Creator will remove the barrier of inhabitation that prevents my kind from outright control of human minds. Do you doubt this? That it is not possible for a being that is half spirit and half mortal to influence a susceptible mind and body? What about the willing subject who opens their mind on purpose for invasion? That was common in my time of those working in sorcery. Your own Christian bible describes the mighty Nimrod who communed with the old ones. Complacency has made man reckless. You have stopped following the old ways of the prophets and ignored the Creator."

"You say it is written, but what reliable source foretells the return of your kind who are dead?"

"Mock me at your peril. In the days of my youth, we had a temple for the fallen near Hermon. We had parchments with ancient knowledge written about the end of times and their return to earth. Some of this material dated back before the great flood when the mighty Watchers existed. I saw the writings with my own eyes, and some of these were handed down to my people from the fallen themselves. Most of those documents were destroyed long ago by King David out of fear. There are places in the Egypt desert where his son Solomon traveled that may still contain more of these documents. Perhaps a few exist with your earthly Pope in his treasured archives."

"You knew King Solomon?"

"Yes, Solomon was known and feared throughout the lands. The Hebrew God allowed him magic tokens to control many spirits. Our kind avoided him to remain free from his spells, although he had a few of the weaker of our kind building his temples and palaces."

Ryan fell silent, not wanting to show her fear. She thought of the possibility he described and shuddered.

"It is time to depart. I will let you walk for now, but you must keep up. If others show up and attack, I will kill them. Do not interfere."

# Chapter Thirteen

# Away from the Chase

**T**HE DNA TEST SAMPLE **from the United States** arrived at the private genetics' lab in Germany. The lab team did not understand the history of the test subject but knew its importance for the group's mission. The team was excited for the arrival of their new director from the United States. Soon they would start the next phase of their most important work.

Nearby, the council was meeting to discuss their next steps.

"Dr. Mullins will arrive tomorrow. He is on the eastern shore of the United States with Gunther. The DNA sample is here. Our technicians assure me the sample arrived safely," van Wilhelm explained to the other council members. He continued speaking.

"The creature is still loose as far as we know, the US authorities are trying to recapture him."

"And if the Americans recapture him?" a council member asked.

"If they do, their plan is to hold him at their Camp Gitmo base in Cuba. We could try and recapture him, but that would be challenging given their security," van Wilhelm explained.

"Can we replicate desirable aspects of the Nephilim then?" another member asked.

"We can do a lot of things. Dr. Mullins explained as a first step he could isolate some of the genes responsible for the extra human abilities. Once that is accomplished, with enough animal experiments they could determine the best way to modify human genes to express these characteristics without undesirable side effects."

"Exactly as you promised then, the chance to live longer and be stronger?" reiterated one of the council members.

"Yes, but we have much work to do before we can try with humans." Responded van Wilhelm.

"Excellent, van Wilhelm. Are there other things Dr. Mullins believes are possible?" inquired the Chancellor.

"We have briefly discussed the concept of cloning. In theory, the Nephilim could be cloned. The biggest challenge is how we control the hybrid once its fully developed. It would be a great asset for the council to have soldiers that could, in essence, be invincible."

"Perhaps with the proper conditioning, a clone such as this could be controlled?" inquired the Chancellor.

"Exactly," explained van Wilhelm. "We have several ways to condition someone. We will discuss further with Mullins. The biggest drawback to not having the hybrid is the lack of ability to question him and gain information. This is a creature who existed during the Roman Empire, who, according to Mullins, existed during the time of King David of Israel. The information we could gain and understand about the fallen would be incredible."

"That is a loss for sure. But there may be other opportunities in the future. The Vatican archives mention spotting these hybrids in various locations around the world. The details are limited, but we know there are possibly others."

"Very true, Chancellor. Our teams continue to research these avenues as well. I plan to greet Mullins tomorrow, and after that we can reconvene to discuss any new information and provide a chance for the group to question him."

"Excellent work, van Wilhelm. One step closer," the Chancellor said confidently.

⊱⊱⊱ ⊰⊰⊰

Back in the United States, the chartered jet carrying Mullins landed in the Portland, Maine, area. Customs needed to be cleared before they could board the plane sent by the council. Mullins took a short walk to enjoy his last view of the States before heading to Europe.

"Gunther, what do you know about the lab we're in route to? I know it's outside of Munich."

"Yes, Dr. Mullins. We have a secure location in a small remote town near a beautiful lake. The lab was set up exactly to your specifications, including the ability to perform gene editing through CRISPR technology. Several of our people live and work there. Outside the lab and living quarters, there is a cattle ranch, vineyard, and restaurant. Security is extremely high, so no one comes in or out without permission."

"And what if I wanted to go into a nearby city for dinner?"

"Occasionally you will be allowed out with an escort. Honestly, you are too important for the project to be let out alone. You should know that by now."

"Yes, just wondering how much autonomy I'll be allowed."

"Not much. We have to focus on the Chancellor's agenda, and the piece you will provide will take us a big step forward. If successful, I think there is a big reward."

"As long as we have the equipment, test subjects, and DNA, then I'm confident of success."

"You will have everything you ask for." Gunther smiled with a malevolent grin. *And so will we*, he thought. He would be watching the Doctor carefully.

~~>>> <<<~~

On the outskirts of Washington, DC, General Briggs met with a group of influential people to discuss the current events. The small group wasn't involved in the current manhunt of Subject Alpha, but they had their own private agenda. The meeting room was sparse, with several men in black suits standing guard inside as well as outside the building.

"Briggs, you assured us the capture of the creature," one of the men said, clearly frustrated by the lack of progress.

"Yes, and that still maybe possible. Both the military and Indian Affairs is tracking it through the mountains. But let's not lose sight of the fact that we now have tissue samples in our possession. We will be able to replicate the DNA and use it as we see fit."

"The sample is in route to our lab location for sequencing and testing. We have two volunteers who are being prepared for the first experiment," reminded an unnamed pharmaceutical executive.

"Excellent progress then," said the senior CIA member standing discreetly in the corner. He was very old school and held a lit cigarette in one hand. "Now, let's talk about one more item of business, the defection of Dr. Mullins and our contingency plan for this."

⤜⤜⤜ ⋘⋘⋘

Later in the afternoon after departing the United States, Mullins sat back in his plush first-class seat as they crossed the Atlantic Ocean. There had been no problems as they completed their customs run. His newly arranged identity and passport worked well. They would arrive in about seven hours in Germany, and then he'd be shuttled to his new villa apartment.

Gunther looked at Mullins while they drank martinis made with Kors Vodka 24k, George V Limited Edition, a special gift from the Chancellor for their return.

"From here, we will address you as Dr. George Schmidt, an American physician with expertise in genetics. You will be introduced to the staff that way, and only a few in security and members of the council will know your real identity. If the staff research your background and ask questions, you will tell them you were working on top secret activities for the United States Government and do not have a public profile," Gunther said. "Study this bio so you will be able to answer questions from your team. They know little about you yet. The test sample arrived today and is being stored until your arrival. After we land and you visit your new quarters, we have a meeting with the council. They are anxious to hear your report and timeline on certain objectives."

"Excellent. What can you tell me about them? Klaus has only provided a few details."

"It is not for me to tell you those details. However, the council consists of the head of five wealthy, powerful families from Europe. They lead our organization, which has been in existence for many years. Their word is law in our organization. As you know, I head our security team and will be assisting you in your research. My team will provide protection for you henceforth."

"Ok. Will we have trouble from outside groups, such as Interpol or the CIA? The military will be looking for me."

"We have eyes everywhere, and we're always watching those groups activities. Interpol and the CIA is suspicious of our group, but certain favors and euros keep us aware of their monitoring, at least for now. We have political friends in high places and a contingency plan if external groups become involved. The biggest thing is for you not to take risks or be visible to prying eyes."

"Understood. You can count on me." Mullins was eager to start over.

It was late evening as their private jet landed without trouble in Munich. As they departed the plane, Gunther breathed in the fresh air. It was good to be back home. The losses had been great, but now was the time to rest, regroup, and plan their next steps. Their destination was about one hundred kilometers away, east near Lake Chiemsee in the state of Bavaria. The compound with the lab was self-contained and allowed easy defense.

An armored car, strategically chosen instead of a helicopter to avoid attention, was waiting for their departure. A heavily armed caravan traveled in front and behind their car. They were not taking any chances with their special guest. Van Wilhelm had been alerted of their arrival and departure from the airport.

"Dr. Mullins, or let me say Dr. Schmidt, how does it feel to be in your new homeland?" Gunther said enthusiastically.

"Fantastic. If this trip is any indication of the life ahead, I'm ready for it. I can't wait to start working on the secrets of the giant."

Mullins enjoyed a glass of wine and plate of cheese they had prepared for him as they drove away. He would have a good night's sleep and then meet with the council early in the morning.

# Chapter Fourteen

# Tamir-Benob on the Run

**W**HITMAN AND HIS TEAM moved **quickly through** the mountains. One of his men had found the giant's tracks and the carcass of the large grizzly his scouts had told him about. This was definitely the handy work of the giant. The bear had been strangled. It would have taken superhuman strength to overpower a thousand-pound bear. There was blood nearby, suggesting a massive struggle. Based on the lack of deterioration of the bear, they were close, perhaps only a few hours behind.

"Mighty Eagle, any word from our scouts?"

"No, Ironhorse, this is worrisome. Something must have had happened. I sent two more men ahead to look for them and the creature."

"Our search helicopter is out and so are the militaries heat-sensing drones. We'll find something soon. The military just confirmed that they're sending troops onto the reservation. IA gave permission, and they're declaring an emergency. It'll be another day or so at best before they reach this area."

"This is getting worse. Many men may die, but much of the land will also be destroyed. The tribal elders will be unhappy with this development. I will let them know."

"Practically, this means we have to find him in the next twenty-four to thirty-six hours, or our home will become a war zone."

They pushed their men onward with a grim determination.

>>> <<<

Dr. Ryan was having difficulty keeping up with Tamir-Benob as they continued their walk through the forest. They were climbing in elevation, and the temperature was getting colder.

"We have to go faster woman."

"I can't go faster than this."

"Fine. Rest now and I will gather food, then we will continue." Tamir-Benob took off into the foliage for game and berries without waiting on her response.

Dr. Ryan looked around frantically. There was nothing near to use as a weapon, or at least not small enough to conceal. Maybe she could leave a sign for others who were tracking her? Time to decide—sneak out and risk the wrath of the beast, or take a chance and leave information for her trackers? She had to risk it, although he could return at any moment.

She inched her way back down the trail, about seventy-five feet away from their stopping point. Tempting to just make a run for it from here, but there is nowhere to go in this maze of a forest. Nothing but pine trees around. She took out a small handkerchief and her military ID.

*Wait. What was that?* She heard the sound of footsteps in the distance. He was coming back!

"Get it together soldier," she muttered to herself. She took a few deep breaths, and then, leaning on the last bit of her internal strength, she quickly tied the blue handkerchief to a low hanging tree limb as it would blow in the wind. She placed her ID on a nearby rock in full view, and finally kicked dirt and leaves around to make it look like human activity. Best she could do for now. She turned and quickly made her way back to area where Tamir-Benob had left her. She was out of breath and hoped her red face wouldn't give her away when the giant returned.

There it was again. The brush moved and leaves crunched. She wiped the sweat from her face and prepared for his arrival, but what she saw coming through the brush instead was a large mountain lion.

*First a bear and now a mountain lion? This was getting ridiculous.* She wondered what she had done in her past life to deserve this. If she hadn't been worried about provoking the lion, she would have laughed out loud.

A rich tan color, approximately six feet in length, and weighing well over two-hundred pounds, this thing was a force to be reckoned with. It snarled and circled her, eying her as a predator playing with its prey. Ryan grabbed a nearby stick to use as a weapon. She was determined not to go down this way. She had come too far to be mauled by a mountain lion.

The snapping animal swiped at her with its massive claws, missing her by mere inches as she stepped back. She had read about the presence of mountain lions in Montana but hadn't seen one since she was assigned to the remote base. She swung the stick hard but missed the lion. Ryan mistakenly backed into a tree and now had little room to maneuver. The lion clawed at her again, this time scratching her arm, ripping her shirtsleeve, and drawing blood. The wound was only superficial but stung. She swung again wildly out of instinct, hitting the animal in the head.

She moved quickly to create distance between them, but the lion was already on its feet and in pursuit. Turning to look at the charging lion distracted her momentarily, and she tripped over a rock in her path. As she fell to the ground, the lion pounced and went airborne.

⇝⇝ ⇜⇜

The scouts found Ramos and Running Wolf. Whitman and his team had caught up quickly. Running Wolf's lifeless body was taken down from the tree and someone would take him back for burial. The power used to impale a man on a spear throw was frightening. Whitman felt remorse and responsibility for Running Wolf's death. Ramos was still alive, but in bad shape. He was in and out of consciousness and had numerous broken bones and a concussion. With proper treatment, he probably would survive and hopefully make a full recovery. Two more of Whitman's men would take him back for an IA helicopter medevac.

Angrily Whitman turned to Stone and Mighty Eagle. "I'm tired of the body count going up. This creature will be stopped!" Yelled Whitman.

"We're closing the distance." Replied Stone.

"Not fast enough. If we don't catch him before sunset, he'll be in the caves. The bigger caves connect, and we'll never find him." A determined Whitman said.

"I'm going ahead with Jim Blackhawk. We'll find this thing and slow it down until the main group can catch up," offered Stone.

"That's a dangerous plan. Jim, are you ok with that?" Whitman asked.

"Yes. Stone let's do it. Time to go on offense. Something this big will have left tracks, especially if he has Dr. Ryan with him. If we make contact, we'll call before engaging."

As the men took off on their horses, Whitman arranged for the medevac and prepared the rest of his men to continue on. The trip was beginning to wear on the group. The fatigue, the casualties, and the ruthlessness of how they were beaten was more psychological torture than physical. He hoped going after this creature was not a mistake.

The mountain lion stretched its claws out in anticipation of landing on Dr. Ryan. Just then, out of the brush, Tamir-Benob's large hand caught the lion by the neck in midleap and jerked it down hard to the ground. The lion bounced back up with a roar and leaped toward Tamir-Benob, hitting him in the middle of his chest with all its weight. The lion scratched and clawed at the giant. Tamir-Benob grabbed the lion by its mane as it clawed at his head, drawing more blood. He angrily threw the lion against a tree about ten feet away. The lion howled and limped up, prepared to charge.

Ryan was amazed that Tamir-Benob still had the energy to fight the lion after the intensity of the clashes so far with the soldiers, the Crow warriors, and that enormous bear.

Tamir-Benob picked up a stick and prepared for battle. As the lion bounded forward to attack, the giant swung the stick like a baseball bat and landed a powerful blow to the lion's head, knocking it several feet into the air. The lion now lay dead, and Ryan sat in disbelief.

"Why did you save me?" she said, her voice barely audible.

Tamir-Benob looked at her, puzzled. "I may need you as leverage against the others coming. They are getting closer. We will leave now to make it to the caves."

"Leverage. Of course. I don't think that will work at this point," she said, worried that he might have alterative motives.

Tamir-Benob said nothing. He just picked her up, slung her over his shoulder, and started walking toward the caves.

※≫≫ ≪≪※

After tracking for about an hour, Jim Blackhawk and Stone made a startling discovery—a handkerchief and Dr. Ryan's military identification badge on the trail. They were close and quickly gaining ground. Even more concerning, there was a dead mountain lion with a broken neck in the clearing about thirty yards away.

It was becoming more challenging for Jim Blackhawk to obtain a signal in the forest even with his phone booster. This might be the last call he could make.

"Frank, this is Jim. We're about a mile ahead of you and found Dr. Ryan's security badge and a dead mountain lion."

"Ok, we'll be right there. Any blood?"

"A little on the lion, probably his."

"I'm betting that Dr. Ryan left her badge behind for us to find like a breadcrumb. Looks like our big man isn't developing a good relationship with the local wildlife."

Stone and Jim Blackhawk continued to profile the area while waiting on Whitman. They found large footprints and berries scattered on the ground. Most likely Dr. Ryan had eaten and then been picked up by the giant. Her tracks were next to his and then suddenly disappeared like before. As Whitman and the rest of the team arrived, he saw the mountain lion laying in a lump near Jim. "That's one large lion."

"Yeah, no kidding. He must have put up quite a fight. We did not find anything else. Here is Ryan's identification," Jim said.

"Where was Dr. Ryan's ID found?"

"Over here," Jim said, walking over to the rock and the tree where the handkerchief was tied.

"Yes, this definitely looks like a breadcrumb."

The direction the giant was leading them was further up the mountain toward the Big Ice Cave, a large cave with ice in it year-round. There were other smaller caves nearby. Whitman called the IA helicopter. The medevac stop had been made and the chopper was heading back toward their location. He gave them coordinates to try and cut the giant off from the caves. They might rendezvous at their current speed in the next few minutes. He decided to push his team to try and reach the location to help in any conflict. There was also an update from the military. They were looking for the creature west of their location and boots were on the ground about five miles away from them. Given the terrain, the military would not arrive until tomorrow afternoon, although the helicopters could be there sooner.

"Time to go. We're close." Whitman jumped back on his horse, checked his rifle one more time, and took off.

## Chapter Fifteen
# Near the Ice Caves

T AMIR-BENOB KNEW THEY WERE closing in on him. A cave might provide adequate cover to hide in. Most large caves connected to others, and he could escape if needed. In the distance he heard a buzzing sound in the air. He anticipated it was a war machine, like he saw in his own country. They would conceal themselves and wait to see if it was a flying metal bird.

"What is it?" Dr. Ryan asked.

"Your people are close; it sounds like a flying machine."

"You mean a helicopter? I don't hear it."

"It is there, approaching now. We will take cover until it arrives. I will need a weapon to fight."

This worried Ryan. If Subject Alpha could hear the helicopter, there would be no approach in stealth. She could only imagine what he would do. She would have to find a way to stop him from destroying her only means of escape.

He pushed her into the brush to take cover. While there he grabbed three long thick branches and used his knife to whittle sharp spear points. He found multiple large boulders, to be used as projectiles. Ryan felt sick to her stomach. The giant intended to bring the helicopter down. The scary part for her was that his idea might work. She would have to witness the death of others once again.

'Stop! You can't kill them. Let them go. Just come in and we can talk this through with our military."

The giant just stared at her for a moment and then spoke. "I do not talk to soldiers; your military is hunting me, and I will defend myself. If they shoot at me, they will die, just like others in the past."

"'The helicopter is not shooting at you; it's trying to find us."

"That is the same thing. They scout for us so the others can find and kill me. I will not allow that."

There was no reasoning with him.

The helicopter pilot had been searching for the past hour since he'd dropped off the Crow tribesmen. There was also a soldier onboard who was a trained sharpshooter. If they saw the giant, they had orders to take him out. Unlike military helicopters, the medevac units were not allowed to carry missiles or large guns. The drones had been unsuccessful in finding heat signatures so far, although Whitman's team of trackers suggested they were heading in this general vicinity.

Tamir-Benob studied the helicopter as it came into view. It slowly approached their hiding place. It was smaller in size than others he had seen before. They had not been seen, so he contemplated whether to take the copter down now or wait a little longer. He decided to wait. The helicopter moved past their location on toward the mountain peaks in the distance.

Picking up the three spears, he turned to Ryan. "We walk now in the brush, hidden by the trees. If the flying machine comes back, I may decide to destroy it. Now get moving."

Ryan did not say anything. She started walking along the tree line. For now, she would do as she was told. At least the people in the helicopter were still safe. Unfortunately, they're reprieve likely wouldn't last long.

Whitman was in close contact with the helicopter. The pilot reported no sighting of the giant. Their trackers were close, so the giant was using the forest as cover. Their target was used to evading others. Based on the distance traveled and how fast the Nephilim was moving, the helicopter was probably ahead of their quarry and needed to circle back. If they planned well, they could use the helicopter to slow the giant down and possibly push him back in their direction. He told Stone and Mighty Eagle of his plan. "Air-1 had no sighting of the creature. He probably passed over him. I asked the pilot to drop to a lower altitude at coordinates that would bring him back toward us. I believe he's using the forest tree line to hide. If the bird comes back and flies in a circular perimeter, we may be able to slow him enough to catch up. We should finally get our chance at stopping him."

"Good plan. Now let's execute and take this menace out," Stone said more determined than ever.

In the distance they heard the rotor blades of Air-1.

⋙⋘

Air-1's pilot had seen movement down below—a brief flash of red through the trees. Something big was moving fast.

The pilot radioed into Whitman, who was about a half mile away. "Agent Whitman. We have spotted something. I think it's our hostile. He is hiding amongst the tree line. What are your orders?"

The pilot was aware the giant held a hostage, so they could not fire indiscriminately. They would have to make do with their sharpshooter and his Remington 700P.

"Roger that, Air-1. Can you get closer for a clean shot? We're double-timing it to get there to assist."

The pilot lowered the chopper and hovered a bit to allow for a better shot.

Tamir-Benob had pulled Ryan with him through the forest to avoid detection. He was surprised when the metal bird had turned quickly back toward them. Destroying the flying weapon was now critical to prevent others from finding them. Flying machines had chased him in the past and he knew how to destroy them. They had used large firesticks, which had nearly killed

168

him. He would need to be cautious and use the woman as a shield.

He quickly looked around for weapons and found several medium sized logs and a few large rocks. They would work nicely as projectiles.

Ryan watched again in horror as he gathered makeshift weapons to bring down the helicopter. She grabbed his arm to try and hold him back. "Stop this craziness now! You can't do this!"

He pushed her hard to the ground and spoke harshly to her. "Stay back or you will get hurt. I have no time for this."

She wiped the dirt off her face and jumped in front of him. "You are not going to kill those innocent men."

He growled and hit her hard across the face with the back of his hand knocking her back down. "Try my patience again and it will be much worse."

She held her hand to her swollen lip, as blood trickled down her face. "You will pay for that and the other things you have done," she swore softly, giving him a look of vengeance.

After laying out his armaments, the giant waited for the metal bird to come back in his direction. The helicopter decreased altitude slowly, hovering to allow the crew to search for them.

The giant grabbed Ryan by the neck and dragged her out into the open, using her body as a shield against the attackers. The sniper would not fire with the woman in the way.

"No shot, no shot. Circle back," the sniper said. "He is using her as a shield."

The pilot turned the aircraft around and circled back from behind to get a better angle. The sniper took aim again and looked for a shot.

Tamir-Benob slowly dragged Dr. Ryan back to the brush until they were out of range for the sniper. *This was a fun game.*

⟫⟫ ⟪⟪

Whitman heard the helicopter in the distance and could briefly see it hovering. The pilot had reported their sighting and was trying to take a shot at the giant from a safe enough distance.

"Let's go. We're only a few minutes away. That chopper can't take him alone." Yelled Whitman. "Move people!"

⟫⟫ ⟪⟪

Tamir-Benob threw Ryan to the ground hard and picked up two spears to use as javelins. He peered around a rock and positioned himself between several trees to partially block himself from the soldiers' view.

The sniper took aim and prepared to fire as the helicopter lowered again.

"Hold her steady. I almost have the shot," declared the sniper.

"Roger that."

The giant moved just as the sniper pulled the trigger. The shot went slightly off center, but it still managed to hit Tamir-Benob in the shoulder.

"Raahhh," yelled Tamir-Benob as the bullet pierced his flesh.

They saw him recoil from the hit, but he continued to move. Ryan kicked the giant's leg as he threw a wooden spear. The little bit of distraction caused the spear to just miss the helicopter blades.

"Imbecile, you will be punished for that!" the Giant screamed.

The sniper shot again but missed, as the giant was turning toward the woman. The beast grabbed a large rock in one hand and a spear in the other. He hurled the rock toward the helicopter more as a distraction than an actual effort to take the craft down. The pilot swerved wildly in response.

Tamir-Benob used this opportunity to rifle the thick spear toward the helicopter blades. Contact! Sparks flew and the noise was nearly deafening. The blade wobbled, and the helicopter dropped fast toward the grassy area near where Dr. Ryan was standing.

As the helicopter descended like a rock, the pilot managed one last message out to Whitman, then crashed.

"Air-1 is hit. Making a hard landing. The creature is wounded."

Ryan covered her eyes as the helicopter smashed into ground with a loud boom and caught fire. The sniper and pilot limped out of the wreckage just before the cockpit was engulfed in flames.

Tamir-Benob ran toward the soldiers, who recoiled in fear.

Ryan chased after him but couldn't catch him. "Come back here you abomination." she called after him to no avail.

The sniper pulled a pistol to shoot, but the giant grabbed his wrist, snapping it in his grasp.

The man let out a scream of pain. "My arm! Get this monster off me!"

Tamir-Benob tossed the sniper toward the crash with such force that his neck broke when he landed. The giant then backhanded the pilot and watched with amusement as he fell to the ground unconscious.

Ryan was appalled at what she had just witnessed. She wanted to stop this madman but couldn't. "You murderer. You just killed two defenseless men."

Ignoring her and satisfied that the soldiers would bother him no more, he turned, picked up Ryan, and began to walk off toward the slope of the mountain in the direction of more caves. He moved fast to put distance between him and the trailing soldiers.

In the distance Whitman and the others saw the chopper go down and heard a loud crash. He knew the sniper made one targeted hit that only slowed the creature down. Whitman and his team quickly made their way to the crash site where they saw the two men on the ground. The helicopter wreckage was engulfed in flames and black smoke was rising high into the air like a smoke signal for the reinforcements they hoped would arrive in time.

"The sniper is dead, no pulse. The pilot has a weak pulse, but we need to get him medical attention now," Whitman said.

"I'm calling the military helicopters with our coordinates for a medevac. We don't have the supplies to help him here," Stone confirmed.

One of the men would stay to meet the reinforcements, although in a few hours it would get dark and that would slow things down. They had closed the gap, but they were still behind and would have to go on foot soon because the terrain would be too difficult for the horses. Several caves were nearby, and the prospect of entering a cave at night to engage this creature was less than desirable. Most likely they would have to go a few more hours, then find a spot to camp and allow the men a much-needed rest.

⠿⠿⠿ ⠿⠿⠿

Tamir-Benob carried Ryan into the mountain terrain for close to two hours before stopping. There was a comfortable distance between him and the soldiers now, although the warriors chasing them were slowly gaining ground. Eventually they would battle, but it would be at a time and place of his choosing, not theirs. This was too reminiscent of the period with David and his mighty men. He remembered one particular event vividly.

"Saul, why will you not face me? Are you not the mighty king of these weak sheepherders? Do you not have a single man with courage? Are you all cowards? Has your God forsaken you? There are no prophets to warn me away. I spit on your name and your God! Face me!" his uncle had taunted.

The mocking had gone on for days.

Tamir-Benob remembered his last conversation with his uncle. "Why, Uncle, do you taunt them such? Are these not the people of the Creator, and our cursed enemy? Why give them anger and courage for a fight?"

"Tamir-Benob, you welp of an offspring. How many have you killed in battle? What do you know of the ways of war? Our kind are meant to rule with an iron hand and without mercy. I taunt them because I can. I taunt them because I am a firstborn of a fallen, and a giant. No one from this tribe of lambs can defeat me. Now go back and do your duties before I show you, my hand. Never question me again."

The next morning had been foggy and was followed by a chilly day; it had rained the night before. The seers had foreseen death and destruction.

Goliath had taunted Saul once again. He was full of wine, and especially loud. However, this time a youth answered his call. Goliath was surprised when the teenager, barely four cubits and a span, addressed him.

"I answer your call," the boy had said.

"What do we have here? A babe, a child? You offend me, Saul. You send a boy to do a man's work. What is your name, whelp?"

"My name is David ben Yishai. The Lord is with me. You should depart and leave our land forever before I smite you."

"Ha ha ha. Saul, this boy has more courage than your entire army. Maybe he should be king instead of you? Do you know, boy, what risks you are entering? When I kill you, we will take your land, your riches, and your women. Your body will be fed to the dogs later today. Perhaps you should run along and let the cowardly king face me."

"I challenge you, unclean abomination. You are an afront to the Most-High. I am not afraid of you. The Lord will protect me as he has against the others. If you are not afraid to fight, then face me, or surrender and leave. I will not give you another chance."

Tamir-Benob recalled the look in David's eyes that day. They were steel, with resolve and without fear. Similar to the warrior chasing him now.

"It is good you have faith in your God, as you will die now, young one."

David pulled a simple pebble out of his pocket, like what one would find in a streambed. He had a small slingshot; many a youth used them back then.

Goliath raised his large sword in one hand. With his other he waived the boy toward him. Goliath laughed and looked to his men. He was more interested in taunting and making the young David look bad. He slipped in the wet grass but caught his footing, still laughing and circling David, not paying any attention. David had studied Goliath, as the giant turned his head to make jokes to his men.

David raised his slingshot and aimed for the giant's forehead, ready to let the pebble go as soon as Goliath turned back. There was tremendous velocity when the pebble hit. Goliath stumbled again, this time falling and hitting his head on a nearby rock.

David quickly approached Goliath and grabbed his sword. The oversized sword was much too heavy for the boy, and it took multiple attempts for him to raise it.

"For my God!" he shouted, and with that young David took Goliath's head.

Goliath had underestimated the determination and speed of his opponent. If he had struck first and focused less on taunting David, the outcome might have been different. After that defeat, the Philistia army collapsed, and the Israelis expanded their control. Within a few years Tamir-Benob was forced to leave the area, and once David became king, he made it his mission to rid the land of Tamir-Benob's kind.

He would not underestimate this warrior; he would strike first. As they moved upward, Tamir-Benob looked for a location to stop for the night. They were on the mountain's forest side near a lake, and there were no caves close to them. His preternatural vision allowed him to see the wolves across the pond. They were warily keeping their distance. The first stars were out now, so those tracking him would stop for the evening. That would allow planning of next steps and a possible ambush to slow them down. Since he did not require much sleep, he would double back when the woman was asleep. As he put Ryan down, she slapped him hard.

"You bastard! Let me go. I want no more part of this. I have a life to get back to."

"What you want does not matter. Your people hunt me like an animal. If they continue, I will use you as bait."

"Too many people have died already."

"Your soldiers captured me, experimented on me! I did not start this war. Do you really believe you can meddle with something beyond your control and have no consequences!" he shouted at her, anger rising up from inside. "Man has never learned and has forgotten the lessons of its youth. This drama will play its course."

Ryan glared at Tamir-Benob in disgust. She would make her escape tonight regardless of the consequences.

Tamir-Benob told her to wait near the base of the trees for him to gather more vegetation for their meal. His preference was meat, but he knew the woman would not eat unless it was cooked. He did not go far in his search for food as he anticipated the woman would run if she had the chance. He would need to watch her closely.

Ryan would be forced to use leaves for bedding like before. She was getting tired of sleeping on the ground, finding makeshift latrines, and missed the simple things like a hot shower and a warm bed.

After a meal of plant leaves, berries, and roots, Ryan laid down to sleep without speaking to the giant. He stood watch while she slept, pondering his next steps. No signs of the soldiers, but plenty of other predators lurking in the forest, wondering who had invaded their domain.

Whitman's team bedded down for the night. He needed to do something to change the dynamic. Everything had been defensive so far. They hadn't built a fire overnight and they were still downwind from their quarry, so hopefully they had remained undetected. After an MRE, a typical military prepackaged food, he explained his plan to the group. Following a short nap, he would go with Jim Blackhawk and Stone to scout for the giant. He wanted to try and find Ryan while the giant was stopped and unaware. They were only a mile or so away from them and might catch them by surprise. Hopefully, they could take her away safely, and then go into phase two—capture or kill the beast. His team would trail behind a little later. At a minimum he wanted to put the giant on defense. With only the light of the moon overhead, he shut his eyes for some much-needed rest. Others on the team took shifts on patrol to make sure the giant did not circle back and catch them off guard.

# Chapter Sixteen

# Council of Five Meeting

I T WAS EARLY MORNING in Germany. The previous night Mullins had enjoyed a meat-heavy meal, a little too much European red wine, and had slept comfortably in his new luxury accommodations overlooking the lake. He was provided with a new ensemble of clothes.

Mullins arrived early to the lab before breakfast to take a quick peak at his new lab. His new assistant was waiting on him.

"Dr. Schmidt, I am Inga and will show you the lab facilities prior to your meeting with the council." Inga was a middle-aged petite woman, professionally dressed in a navy jump suit peering at her clipboard with stylish glasses and brown hair pulled back in a ponytail.

Inga led him down a long corridor with stainless steel doors lining both sides. Some had small windows so you could see inside. The main lab required both a retinal scan and ID badge for entrance. State of art equipment has been set up, including a surgical suite. As they walked through Mullins gave his approval.

"Thank you, Inga. I would like to see the cold room first, where the recently arrived test samples are being housed."

As Mullins examined the new expansive facility, Gunther made his way to retrieve the doctor for the council meeting.

Giovanni was waiting for them as they entered the room. The traditional European breakfast and coffee was laid out for them. Mullins enjoyed the aroma of the Italian blend before sitting down. The serene lake could be observed out the numerous floor-to-ceiling windows, which took up an entire wall of the room.

"Do you have your notes? Please let me know if you will you require anything else," Gunther asked.

"Thank you, Gunther. I'm ready to begin."

The was set up with video camera to allow live feed. The conference table and plush chairs would have allowed at least ten to sit comfortably. In the corner was a gas fireplace, with a small lit flame.

As the three men took their seats, the camera came to life with all the members of the council staring intently out at Mullins.

"Good morning, Dr. Mullins. It is good you arrived safely. I hope you find your accommodations satisfactory?" van Wilhelm inquired.

Mullins answered, trying to sound calm even though he was bouncing his right leg rapidly under the table. He'd waited so long for this moment. "Very satisfactory and much appreciated."

"The council is eager to speak with you today." After brief introductions, van Wilhelm addressed the likelihood of other hybrid beings and next steps, and then Mullins took questions from the council.

"Does the US military think there are there more of his kind? The Vatican seems to think so?" Liza Agosti, a senior council member from Italy with ties to the Pope, asked.

"Yes, Ms. Agosti they do. Reports from different regions of the Middle East suggest there are more of these creatures running around. But this was the first of its kind captured by US forces. US intelligence believes the hybrids have migrated to the caves due to all the fighting, to avoid detection. I'm told that's one reason they used MOAB bombs—they were trying to take out a nest of them. From what we can tell, the creatures are not running in clans but as individuals spread out over the area. Most likely the military will continue its search for other test subjects secretly," Mullins continued. "There have been unsubstantiated reports of these type of hybrids in the United States, and Native American legends from hundreds of years ago in different regions suggest these creatures may have migrated there many years ago. Can you share what the Vatican thinks?"

"We have found limited information in their archives, but it is possible more is contained in other remote church locations. They report interactions primarily in the Middle East similar to the US military as well as in Northern Africa. The Church has tried to exterminate their kind over the years. They have sent emissaries out occasionally to hunt them down with some success, although at the cost of many human lives. They had a second line of research that focused on the theory of disembodied spirits of the Nephilim. There is some thought that spirits of the dead giants still roam the earth looking for host bodies to inhabit. Although the Vatican papers suggest that the spirits cannot inhabit a body with a soul unless invited in or they may possibly take possession of a body that is inanimate, our research has not substantiated this. The Vatican does have an archaeological division that focuses on mainstream research, but they do not have an active dedicated team researching this topic, at least not for the last hundred or so years," suggested Council Member Agosti.

"The copied parchment you have from the cave mentions the Knights Templar hunting the creatures and their general hate of the Church and its emissaries. We can assume there has been a long history of, shall we say, unpleasant interactions with the Church and its agents," Mullins reminded them.

"Although I believe it is fairly obvious at this stage, can you explain to the group what the US military was hoping to accomplish with the subject and how far along are they in their work?" interjected van Wilhelm.

"We had some successes with pharmaceutics and considered robotic enhancements. But this would be our first true major biological breakthrough. We had plans to insert new gene capabilities into soldiers. Just think, a soldier with the capability to see five times further, or one who could hear an enemy coming a mile away. A second strategy would have been eventual cloning, but there would have been the issue of how to control the developed clone.

"Our plan had been to try to gain some preliminary information from the beast and then send him to a secure location in Guantanamo Bay in Cuba. He proved to be highly intelligent, learned English quickly, but he was very devious and eventually escaped after killing many US soldiers. So, the US military is in preliminary stages of their research. They have a much simplistic way of looking at this opportunity."

"After the creature escaped, how was your interaction with him as well as our security team?" van Wilhelm asked.

"It was all very brief. The creature's escape from our compound gave the needed distraction to secure the sample and meet with your courier. Once the creature left the compound, Dr. Ryan, a physician on the project, and I went to the American Indian reservation area, which has many mountains and forests, to lend support to the US military. It was fortunate that as we made our way Gunther and Giovanni approached us, with the creature following closely behind. I did not realize at the time that your team had already encountered him. The Nephilim killed a US security member, so when the beast came out of the woods, I offered up Dr. Ryan as a trade in order for us to escape."

"Why do you think he accepted your offer?" an unknown council member asked.

"During our initial interactions at the US compound, Dr. Ryan and the subject had a very contentious verbal interaction. I thought he wanted revenge on her, and it seemed like a logical trade. The creature didn't kill her outright, and given his aggressive personality, I'm assuming he plans to either use her as a bargaining chip or to have her as a mate to sire future offspring. His parchments mentioned wanting to repopulate his kind in the future and attacking man," Mullins explained.

"Interesting, so we don't know the current where abouts of the creature or this Dr. Ryan?"

"No, my last communication suggested that multiple teams were hunting him, from the military to the local law enforcement. Eventually they will bring helicopters in with missile capability, and they will find and destroy him. He is resilient, but I doubt he would survive an attack like that."

"I would expect as much; this is very insightful. Now let us discuss our research and your plans here. Can you lay out to the council the key projects over the next twelve months, and when we can consider human testing?" van Wilhelm asked.

'Those questions are difficult to answer just yet. Technically we must perform genetic sequencing to look for unknown genes in the creature and compare the sequence of similar existing genes and determined which are expressed. We have a rather good idea of which gene clusters are involved in strength, tissue regeneration, and other key characteristics. However, there may be genetic material found only in the hybrid from its nonhuman heritage. We now have CRISPR gene editing technology, and once we identify the appropriate genes to alter, we should be able to make modifications in future human DNA. If there are any nonhuman genes identified, we should be able to use viral vectors to add those to humans in the future.

Of course, we will perfect all of that first in animals, as we need to make sure there are no undesirable side effects. With hybrid DNA, we don't know for sure what to expect with animals. Maybe even a lion man out of Moab? Lots of possibilities, but at a minimum we will need the next year or more for genetic testing and to begin animal trials.

Obviously with more resources we can do this much quicker. The other question is whether to alter adults or start in childhood during early development, but both should be possible."

"Which gene editing approach do you recommend first?" asked the Chancellor.

"We plan to focus on several areas simultaneously. Our first targets will be strength, endurance, tissue regeneration, and longevity. Secondary genes will be linked to hearing, vision, and smell."

"And your opinion on cloning?" chimed in van Wilhelm.

"Mr. van Wilhelm, cloning is one option, but not ideal in my opinion. Unless we can figure out how to accelerate aging, the clone would be born a child and we would have to wait several years for it to grow into adulthood. We then would have the issue of making sure the clone was controllable. Perhaps that would be a second development option long-term, once our members have been enhanced and life spans are longer for us, and once we need additional soldiers."

"That makes sense. There is much to contemplate. We have assembled your new staff for a meeting with you later today. No one on the lab team knows your real identity, and we would like to keep it that way. You will have maximal resources, and we will speak weekly on progress," van Wilhelm concluded.

⟫⟫⟫ ⟪⟪⟪

Mullins's staff were bright and enthusiastic. Everything in the lab was as specified. Emil, a senior scientist, was providing a tour of the remainder of the facility not viewed early in the morning.

"The one area we haven't visited is the holding area. We have prepared this area for primates, but below ground is a stronger concrete reinforced section which can be used if human test subjects were involved," Emil explained.

"Excellent, and has the area been tested already?" Mullins asked.

"Not yet, but it was built to your specifications and should hold the strongest creature. Gunther oversaw additional security measures as well."

"Do we have volunteers for testing?"

"Yes, more than needed. We are ready to move to human tests when you are. We do not have to worry about those pesky ethics committees like in America."

"That is good news. Now let's go back over the project plan."

Gunther put their enhanced security surveillance plan in place. They expected greater scrutiny from the outside since word was making its way around that the American scientist was missing. Besides alphabet sounding groups, others from eastern countries would be watching closely. He would expect a hefty price tag on Mullins head. How many geneticists with expertise in Nephilim biology and genetic engineering could there be?

# Chapter Seventeen

# Back in the Montana Forest

IT WAS LATE IN the evening and Ryan was sound asleep.

Few stars were out, and it was a chilly night. The giant could see his breath in the air.

Tamir-Benob decided to assess how close the soldiers tracking him were. He would go a mile or so in search of them. If there were sentries, he might kill them now to create confusion. He walked away under the moonlight, making little sound as he crept through the forest. He carried a spear and knife on his hunt. There was no scent of the others. They must be staying downwind. The forest was full of wildlife; he passed a fox, a few snakes, and some other creatures of the night as he surveyed the area. His built-in night vision allowed clear sight as he made his way toward the men.

Whitman and his two comrades left in the direction of where they thought the giant waited. Armed with night vision goggles, they still felt at a disadvantage in such a remote area with little other light to guide them.

"We need to take a wide route to avoid any chance encounters. Jim, take point," Whitman whispered. The men nodded in agreement.

Before long the group picked up the giant's track, but something caught Jim Blackhawk's attention. They were north of the giant's trail, moving in a parallel direction. Something big was moving quietly through the woods, but every now and then it stepped on a twig.

"Stop. Take cover now," Blackhawk said softly, motioning to the others with hand signals to get behind the trees.

They found hiding places and listened as the movement got closer. A large, red-haired man slowly came into their view. The creature moved with little noise, cautiously looking around. The men froze to avoid being seen.

Tamir-Benob knew he was close. Others were nearby, in hiding somewhere. The hair on the back of his neck was raised. He paused for a long time, then continued walking.

Whitman felt the danger of being this close to the hybrid in the dense forest. He signaled Stone and Jim Blackhawk to give wide berth to the giant and track from a distance. If the creature did make it to their camp, they would be able to surprise it. He also sent an alert to the men at the camp. They were to quickly break camp and go into hiding on high alert.

Whitman debated on what course of action to take, but this was his best chance so far to find Dr. Ryan—if she was still alive. "I'm going ahead and will try to find Ryan. She can't be that far ahead. Probably our best chance to get her alone. You both keep tracking and don't engage unless he attacks."

⤜⤛⤜⤛

Dr. Ryan woke and discovered her prison guard gone. She had no idea where he went or when he was coming back. She suspected he was out hunting and decided to make a run for it. Many of the stars were covered by clouds, and she was in darkness, except for the light of the moon. She heard the cry of a wolf in the distance. Dr. Ryan quickly laced up her boots, grabbed her jacket, and exited the cave. There was no sight of the beast. She would chance it in hopes that soldiers would be tracking from the direction they arrived.

⤜⤛⤜⤛

As Tamir-Benob moved through the forest, he picked up the scent of man. He moved slowly, surely; he would not find them asleep without a sentry. He made his way into what could have been a camping spot. Although hidden, he saw where men had lain on the ground sleeping and where earth and leaves had been moved back like several had gathered together, perhaps to speak to one another. By the looks of things, they were here recently but had left.

They were most likely watching him from a distance hidden by the dark, and he contemplated whether to search further. He decided now was not the time to engage in battle. Best to go back and plan the encounter. After a long look around, he turned and began to head back toward the cave where he had left Ryan.

Standing atop the adjacent hill over a hundred meters away, Mighty Eagle watched in horror as the hybrid walked away. His night vision binoculars confirmed his fears about his people's legends. The giant knew they were there but purposely refrained from battle. He had to alert Whitman. From the other side of the woods, Stone and Jim Blackhawk watched the giant turn around and begin heading in the other direction. They were confused as to why he was leaving; it seemed like he was aware of the presence of others and was retreating. They were out of sight but would continue tracking him and alert Whitman, so he could get out of the giant's path.

Whitman made it into a clearing near an area that looked like a campsite. Fresh tracks were leading from the area from both the giant and a human. It was likely that Ryan left recently to escape. A bold move.

While looking around, he received texts from both Mighty Eagle and Jim Blackhawk confirming his suspicion. The creature was returning toward the cave, and he had less than ten minutes to catch Ryan before the giant was back. He wasted no more time and took off in a jog in the direction of the human tracks.

~»»» «««~

Ryan moved quickly down the trail. She had a bad  feeling but kept moving forward. No matter what she had to escape this nightmare. She grabbed a sharp stick as a weapon but had little confidence it would help much. She could barely see in front of her and was constantly on the alert for the creature as she made her way back toward the others.

Whitman could easily follow Ryan's trail, as she was not adept at hiding her movement. He was in full-sprint mode trying to make up the distance when he heard someone pushing through the brush ahead. He suspected it was either Ryan or the giant. There was no time to approach in stealth. The creature could be very close.

Dr. Ryan heard the thud of footsteps approaching from behind. Someone was running toward her. The pattern as the footsteps hit the ground was heavy and quick, but lighter and clumsier than the gait she remembered from being carried through the forest by Tamir-Benob. Was it another animal stalking its prey? Another bear or mountain lion, maybe? She looked for a place to hide and hopefully to wait out whatever was coming. She moved behind a large tree and set of bushes for cover and positioned herself so she could see. She gripped her stick turned spear in preparation for the fight.

Just then Whitman moved into the clearing. His night vision goggles had allowed him to detect movement nearby, someone smaller looking around a corner of a Douglas fir. It appeared to be human and was most likely Dr. Ryan.

He spoke out in a whisper to alert her. "Dr. Ryan, is that you? It's Agent Whitman from Indian Affairs? Can you hear me, Kathryn?"

Dr. Ryan was shocked but relieved to hear Whitman's voice. "Agent Whitman, is that really you? I can't believe you're here. I thought you were the giant. He's probably close to us; he could be here at any moment."

"Yes, it's Whitman. My people have eyes on him. He's close to them near our camp, less than a mile south of here. The giant was close to their camp, but at the last minute turned around. My folks broke camp before he arrived, so that probably spooked him. He has uncanny tracking abilities and a sense of things before others. Did he leave you alone back at the cave?"

"We were camping in a clearing last night. He threatened to kill me if I ran away. I was too afraid to try and run in the middle of this wilderness. But after what he did to those men in the helicopter, I had to risk it. He's a monster. How are we going to stop him? I saw him kill a large grizzly bear with his bare hands. And he seems to hate you in particular for some reason—"

"We're going to stop him. The military should catch up tomorrow and bring more firepower. My men will slow him down. More important, are you hurt? Hungry?"

"Hurt no, but starving. Berries and roots are getting old."

Whitman reached into his backpack and handed her a bottle of water, a power bar, and a meal-ready-to-eat honey barbeque chicken sandwich. She ate ravenously.

"You need to finish that while we walk. He's probably trailing closely behind us. Gulp the water so you're hydrated, but don't throw any trash out for him to find," Whitman instructed.

Silently, they started their trek away. Whitman texted both Mighty Eagle and Jim Blackhawk that he had found Ryan and they were heading north away from the giant. His men were trailing their foe and would catch up with him during daylight. They had a plan to engage, but there were a lot of unknowns.

The giant slowly moved toward higher ground. He wanted to assess if he were being followed. The soldiers who watched him approach their camp would have sent scouts to trail him. He may have to circle back around to kill them before heading back. They were testing him.

Jim Blackhawk and Stone were in danger of being detected by the creature. They had made it to higher ground, but the beast was still tracking in their direction. They moved away, but would have to remain motionless after that, lest they give away their location. The waiting game seemed like hours. Thankfully it was still dark.

Mighty Eagle and the remaining men were on the move. He was in deep thought as they moved through the dark waiting for dawn. Although he was a medicine man, and his tribes spiritual guide, this defied everything he understood. The group continued on; they would join up with Stone and Whitman after the creature moved a little further ahead.

Tamir-Benob picked up his pace; he was much faster than a normal man. He would wake the woman and continue to travel north. There were snow peaks and once there it would be impossible for those following to easily catch him. It would be too cold for the woman, but she could serve as a shield if he were attacked.

Something seemed different as he worked his way through the dense foliage. The scent of humans—the female and another ahead. That should not be possible. Had the female left the cave and happened on another human to aide her? His anger increased. He needed to check the campsite and see if she had returned. If she were gone, he would find her and kill her, and whoever was helping.

# Chapter Eighteen

# Preparing for the Final Battle

**G**ENERAL BRIGGS WAS UP **before daylight arranging** for multiple helicopters with rocket launchers and several squads of soldiers heavily armed to meet Stone and the others after daylight. He was giving them time to triangulate where the giant was located and to rescue Dr. Ryan. At this point they had abandoned any hopes of capture. They did have tissue samples and could perform DNA analysis. Since this fiasco had gone on too long, the governor had activated the National Guard, and they would be closing off the perimeter. The biggest problem was going to be keeping the creature from finding a cave to hide in, especially one that connected underground. Drones were already in the air and would coordinate based on Stone's communications.

Whitman and Ryan made steady progress back toward the clearing where Ryan had been staying. He decided to set a trap before continuing. It was about an hour before daylight, and the last several days had taken their toll on Ryan. She needed to stop and take a breather anyway. She pointed out to Whitman where she had been sleeping and the direction she and the giant were heading.

Whitman began to set a trap for the giant in the clearing. He wanted to put the creature on defense for once.

"What are you doing?" Ryan asked.

"I'm laying a surprise for the unfriendly who will soon be catching up to us."

He quickly took out four trip line hooks and two grenades he had obtained from Stone out of his two pack of Kevlar trip line wires.

"See where the trail exits into the clearing where you were camped? His tracks are here and it's the most obvious way he'll return to the clearing to see if you're here. I'm placing two trip wires with grenades to cover those areas," Whitman continued.

He attached the wire to the grenade pen and then to nearby trees to hold everything in place. Then he lowered the wires to around ankle level. "It will most likely still be dark when he comes through here. Given he knows others are chasing from behind, he'll be in a rush to find you and leave. A normal person would be killed by the blast, but he'll only be hurt and angry.

It should at least slow him down a bit. We may even hear the detonation."

"What if your men come here first? Is it smart to make him angry?" Ryan asked.

"I'll let them know about the trip wires when we leave. Normally I would not want to rile him up, but this will give him a little pause that we're fighting back and will make him hesitate when we see him again. Now it's time to get moving."

They left heading north for the peaks in the distance. And for the first time, Ryan felt a little better about their chances of survival.

⤜⤜⤜  ⤛⤛⤛

Stone and Jim Blackhawk had rejoined the main group as they tracked the progress of the giant. Two of their men were ahead scouting, but still far enough behind to not be detected by the beast.

They had received word from Whitman of the trip wire and their plans to move toward the Great Ice Cave. That would be a good rendezvous location for the military. They only had seven men left in their group, including the scouts, because two of their men had to wait with the downed pilot and sniper.

Whitman anticipated they were an hour away on foot from the big Ice Cave. They could stop there.

"There's a sizeable cave an hour or so away from here. There's a back entrance on the other side of the mountain. It could allow us to put distance between us and the giant."

"Can we beat him there?" Ryan asked.

"Yes, we should be able to. And if he does follow us, that might allow my men to come up from the rear. It might be just enough time for the military to catchup."

"Let's do it."

As the pair continued on, Whitman still wondered about Dr. Mullins. Once they had a moment to speak further, he would ask Dr. Ryan about what happened.

"Once the giant finds you missing and trips the trap we set, he'll follow us. Did he speak to you at all? Tell you, his name?"

"Tamir-Benob was the name he used," she replied.

"When Tamir-Benob follows us to the cave, our plan will be to lure him in. We'll destroy the back exit when we leave so he can't follow us. If all goes well, when he tries to exit the cave, my men will be there to stop him."

"If all goes well?"

"Yes, I would prefer to destroy the beast with fire to keep the military from getting their hands on him. Who knows what will happen if the military gets ahold of him again?"

Ryan felt bad for the part she had played in this endeavor. Her team had been so idealistic, and to think Dr. Mullins was playing them all along. The least she could do was stop this creature and prevent the military from continuing their research.

"And if he catches us in the cave?" she asked.

"I would prefer that not to happen, but if he does, we'll push him back with small arms fire, lay a few more traps, and use trickery since he doesn't know the cave well enough to slip out."

Ryan wasn't optimistic but felt an obligation to see it through.

The giant made it back to his previous campground. Slowly he moved through the foliage, detecting the scent of the woman and another. He did not hear or see any movement ahead and suspected they had fled.

As he stepped forward, his ankle tripped a small wire. He saw a bright flash from the corner of his eye, then pain radiated up his entire body. He was thrown into the air by the force of the blast. Most of the pain was in his chest and face. As he tried to stand, he felt something warm and wet. He looked down to see that he was covered in blood. There was a loud ringing in his ears. He had been thrown at least ten feet from the blast. Someone had found his campground in the dark, taken the female, and set a trap for his return. His anger grew as he recovered. This had to be the work of the warrior who drew first blood. He would catch them. He needed a moment to catch his breath. *Finally, a worthy opponent.*

In the distance, Whitman heard the blast. "Kathryn, did you hear that? We have maybe three quarters of a mile lead on the giant. He probably won't be stunned for long, so we need to try to add to our distance."

"How close are we to the entrance to the cave?"

"It's just a few minutes away. We have to go down a path to find the entrance, but it should be less than ten minutes from here."

Stone and the Crow warriors trailing the giant heard the blast as well. They looked at one another, and for the first time felt more confident. Ironhorse had drawn first blood and really injured the creature. Daylight was peeling off in the distance, and the chase was on.

⟫⟫⟫ ⟪⟪⟪

Before approaching the cave Whitman put on his night vision goggles and gave Ryan his pullover jacket to keep her warm. They followed the trail down about hundred yards and then reached the cave entrance.

"We made it. He'll have to come this way to enter the cave. That'll give us the advantage," Whitman noted.

"If you say so," Ryan replied, less confident in the plan than Whitman.

201

He handed Ryan a flashlight and they entered together. Although the general public could enter this area, the terrain made it difficult to access, and there were no lights or other manmade objects left in the cave. They stopped and he pulled out of his pack a military-grade infrared motion sensor that he linked to his wristwatch.

"If anyone enters here, we'll know. This will give us a heads up of any unexpected company."

They continued on, winding their way further into the cave.

"As a youth I used to come here against my father's wishes," Whitman explained. "He thought it was dangerous to be here. But I learned a lot about caves, especially this specific cave. This one goes on for about a mile with a stream and some ice due to the temperature. There are some false exits and one side cavern that's about thirty-by-thirty feet with a small exit. The exit enters the forest about two miles from here. Lots of wildlife use this cave, so don't be alarmed by the bats. Bigger animals should avoid us."

They moved further into the cave, then stopped to set another trap. Ryan looked up and saw the bats hanging on the ceiling and imagined them leaving in swarms at night to hunt. She hoped to be gone by then, but she knew any noisy activity would send the bats flying all around.

"This surprise will be a little more dangerous for our friend—another trip wire. Positioning it to a small stick lever below a large boulder up there will do the trick. This is probably a thousand-pound boulder. When the wire is tripped, the boulder will roll down right for him."

Ryan watched in amazement as Whitman set it up. "Did the military teach you this?"

"Some of this I learned in the service; other stuff I was taught growing up. We had to work with the land provided. This will slow him down, but it should also make enough noise to warn us as he gets closer."

The pair kept going until they finally found the side room with exit that Whitman described. Based on the rocks piled up and dirt present, the room had not been visited in some time.

"In the back corner there's a tunnel that leads out. It's small, but there's enough room to get through and in about thirty feet it leads out near a set of bushes that hide the exit. Hang tight for a minute and I'll be right back." Whitman disappeared quickly, leaving Ryan feeling exposed. She knew she was overreacting, but she was still nervous being alone knowing the injured giant was on his way there now.

Tamir-Benob was up and moving again quickly toward the cave. Their tracks were fresh, and he was only minutes behind them. He came out of the forest and looked down several yards to what appeared to be a cave entrance. This puzzled him. Why would the warrior enter a cave unless it was a trap for him? He did not sense any others around, but he was mindful of the soldiers tracking him. Cautiously Tamir-Benob made his way down the path to the cave entrance.

Whitman's team was making their way quickly toward their anticipated encounter. They had lost contact with Whitman after he entered the cave. Everyone felt a final showdown was coming as daylight came through the trees. They passed the clearing where the grenade exploded and knew their destination was less than a mile away.

"This is Stone. Confirm coordinates for mission drop zone. Over."

Whitman popped back out of the small door-sized hole and startled Ryan. "You scared me half to death!"

"Sorry about that. The exit is clear, and we are good to go on our end."

He pulled out two sticks of dynamite with detonating cord hanging low and a lighter.

Ryan's eyes grew large. "You're full of tricks, aren't you. What's that for?"

"Timing will be critical, but when we leave, I want to collapse the tunnel. It's small, but with enough effort he may make it through the opening. Collapsing the tunnel will force him to go back to the front of the cave to exit, and by then reinforcements will be there. Although, this is the last of our weapons."

Ryan was doing her best, knowing they were serving as bait for the bigger team.

The giant entered the cave from the front entrance just as Whitman and Ryan had earlier. He knew they were close. The scent of the woman and warrior were strong. He would go in, kill them, and leave before the others arrived. The darkness and the similarities to his cave back home were comforting to him. He walked in slowly and unknowingly tripped the motion detector. His enhanced night vision allowed him to see normally, but he hadn't noticed the wire.

Further back in the cave, Whitman and Ryan had been talking more about her encounter with the giant. She told Whitman that Tamir-Benob had described his history as a product of fallen angels and that he had witnessed the battle of David and Goliath of biblical times and many other famous military generals from history.

Just then, Whitman's watched beeped alerting him of the arrival of the giant.

"Is that what I think it is?" Ryan asked.

"Unfortunately, yes. He's in the cave."

Fear ran down her spine. Whitman had set up a fortified position near the entrance to the exit room. They were concealed behind rocks, and they had multiple guns, including a rifle laid out and loaded.

"I don't see how it could have been anything else. I don't think a large animal would come into the cave during daylight hours, especially given the amount of human activity here.

Unfortunately, there's no way to contact the others, but I'm confident they're close. The grenade would have alerted them, and they have the coordinates of the cave. We must be calm, engage him briefly, and then escape out the back."

"Sure you don't want to leave right now?" Ryan asked.

"If we leave now, he may escape, and he could even track us down. No, we need to bait him and pull him back here for a bit. If you'd rather, just go ahead and leave out the back and wait on me outside. I can engage him here."

"No, I'm all in," Ryan said with a smile. There was something about Whitman that made her more confident. He was strong, intelligent, and honest. In this life-threatening situation, he came across as protective and that was attractive to her. *Maybe in another life they could have been something more.*

⟫⟫ ⟪⟪

The tired warriors arrived at the entrance of the cave. The giant had left tracks along the way.

"It looks like he passed through here just moments ago. Let's start on the fortification as planned. We probably don't have very long," directed Mighty Eagle.

As one group worked at the entrance, several other members went inside to scout—an extremely dangerous mission. There was no way to know for sure that Whitman and the military doctor were inside, but Mighty Eagle and the warriors had to assume they were. Mighty Eagle felt his ancestors would have had similar fears.

The team quickly set up special high temperature fire logs to start the blaze in anticipation of their battle with the creature. Several tribesmen quickly brought dry firewood to help. The timing to start the fire would be crucial. More men were preparing to go in to keep the giant from escaping.

Whitman and Ryan were on a ledge waiting for the giant to arrive. They knew he was going slow on purpose to prolong the wait, and their anxiety. It was now a battle of two wills, and Whitman was determined to win.

"He'll be here soon," whispered Whitman.

"I know, I can hear something coming," A fearful Ryan agreed.

The human scent was strong as Tamir-Benob made his way through the cave. He had crossed a stream and was back on a narrow trail. He studied the cave as he walked, spear in hand. As he stepped down, he tripped a small wire. A large boulder started rolling toward him. He managed to stop the boulder with some effort and then pushed it aside. Irritation rose in him again, as the sound of the rock smashing against a wall reverberated throughout the cave. The warrior had set this trap and now knew his location.

"Arrgggghhhhh!" The beast roared with fury as a warning to the warrior.

Whitman and Ryan shuddered at the shear ferocity of the sound as it echoed through the tunnels and into the room where they hid.

"You can do this," Whitman assured Ryan. "I'm going to slow him down."

Whitman and Ryan saw the giant come into view as they spied on him from up top. Although dark in the cave, it was still light enough to see his imposing frame coming. The sheer size of the being was incredible. Tamir-Benob did not see them as he made his way toward the end of the cave. Whitman aimed his .308 Winchester with night vision scope at the giant's chest. As Tamir-Benob turned, Whitman fired two quick shots, knocking the giant down. The gunshots sounded like a bomb exploding in the cave. Ryan picked up a weapon in anticipation of needing to fire soon.

Stone and Jim Blackhawk heard the shots fired and knew the sound meant Whitman was engaging the giant. They wanted to help. The beast would take an army to kill. Stone grabbed his M136 AT4 anti-tank missile and turned toward Blackhawk. "Get that fire started. I'm going to try to take him out with the rocket. Do not wait on me. The military has our coordinates. Helicopters are thirty minutes out."

Tamir-Benob yelled in pain and looked upward toward Whitman and Ryan. His eyes burned bright orange with rage. He saw the warrior and the woman both armed with firesticks looking down at him. Their flashlights lit the cavern. Finally, he was face-to-face with his nemesis.

"Warrior, tell me your name. I want to know who has brought down my wrath!"

Whitman shot him a stern glare and said, "Tamir-Benob, you challenge Ironhorse Whitman, son of Running Water Whitman of the Apsáalooke Crow Nation."

"Ironhorse, you know my name," he said, throwing a rock toward Whitman. It careened off the wall, breaking into pieces but showing the giant's strength. "In my day, knowing someone's name allowed you power over them. But that is not the case anymore, is it?"

"Giant, what do you seek? Surely something more besides battle? Answer that."

Using this exchange as a chance to catch his breath and wait on his wounds to heal, he responded, "I will answer you, as you have proven worthy of a reply. My kind has for thousands of years lived in the shadows. But before the great flood we ruled the world and did as we pleased. Mortal men feared us. Our ancestors were fallen spirit men, and because of that we are superior to the Adam man in every way. For many years after the flood, we were the men of renown. Your historians called us Greek gods, Roman gods, and other deities in various cultures. It is our destiny to take back this world. I intend to lead more of my kind back. Your army thought they could hold me. There will be no accommodation for that insult. You and everyone here will shed blood for that affront. Then I will go back to my homeland and build a new army."

"I can't allow you to do that."

"And how will you stop me? You are a brave warrior, but still a mortal man."

"Didn't the Hebrew mortal King David stop your kind with just a slingshot and small rock?"

"David was helped by the Hebrew God. And Goliath made mistakes. I will not make those same mistakes with you."

"Maybe you should have thought about that before coming up here. If not me, the US military will not let you leave this mountain. We have better weapons than sling shots and rocks, and many fine warriors. You will be dead before the end of this day," Whitman said, trying to stall for time.

Ryan whispered to Whitman, "You're making him mad. Is that a good idea?"

Whitman ignored her and continued to bait the beast.

Stone had moved to the perimeter and could see the large red-headed giant looking up at Whitman. He needed to get a little closer to fire his weapon. He debated lighting his flare but didn't want to give away his advantage.

Whitman noticed Stone approaching and was trying to draw the giant's attention. "Tamir-Benob, my people have fought your kind before. Many years ago, your brothers were here and tried to destroy my people and take our land. Our warriors killed your kind then. That is about to happen again."

"Your tribe may have killed some of my kind, but none were as strong as me. The land will run red with the blood of your people and the soldiers who are with them," Tamir-Benob warned.

Stone approached closely. As the giant turned toward him, he fired and caught the beast by surprise. Tamir-Benob was hit and flew back against the wall unconscious. Stone then quickly made his way up the rocks to where Whitman and Ryan stood.

"I'm assuming that didn't kill him?" Whitman asked.

"I don't think so, but it bought us some time while the men are readying the fire in front of the cave. How are you doing Dr. Ryan?"

"I'll live. Just wanting to get out of here. Glad you're here, but that was a risky move," she said.

"Stone, what are you going to do now?" Whitman asked.

"Going back to the front of the cave to help Mighty Eagle and the group. Assuming your plan works, the giant will have to come through us to leave. I have the anti-missile gun again if needed, and Mighty Eagle is preparing a fire to greet him."

"Alright, Kathryn. Time for us to go. We need to be gone when that thing wakes up," Whitman said. "Stone, thanks for coming in, but you've got to make your exit. The others will need you at the front."

"Ok, catch you on the outside. Rangers led the way!" He took off in a jog, giving the giant one last glance. Best to move; the giant was waking up.

A minute or so later, Tamir-Benob rolled over slowly, unable to get up just yet, but murmuring softly.

"Move Kathryn, he's already waking up," Whitman said.

Needing no further encouragement, Ryan made her way toward the room with the second exit.

They quickly left the cave through the small passage. After he got Ryan safely outside, Whitman went back in to set the dynamite and collapse the tunnel. He found the location where the dynamite would cause the most damage and lit the long fuse. There wasn't a lot of time to ensure his estimates were correct, so he made his best guess. He sprinted out of the exit passage right before the explosion. There was a flash of light, billowing smoke, and gravel shooting in all directions. The blast was powerful enough to knock Whitman down as he exited the cave. Ryan ran over to make sure Whitman wasn't injured in the blast.

## Chapter Nineteen

# Reckoning in the Cave

**S**TONE SPRINTED OUT OF the front of the cave as the men were laying wood stacks near the entrance. Mighty Eagle turned to speak with Stone while still giving orders to his men. They had quickly built up a solid wall and were preparing to light the high temperature logs to accelerate the burn and increase the temperature inside.

"We heard the anti-tank gun. Did you do much damage? Is Ironhorse ok?" Mighty Eagle asked.

"They were as safe as could be expected. Apparently, Dr. Ryan escaped on her own and then Whitman found her in the woods. They were able to keep just ahead of him. I caught the giant by surprise. The shot injured him but probably only made him angry enough to follow me out here. Whitman and Ryan were heading out the back while the giant was down. Whitman's going to use dynamite to collapse the exit. We have a few minutes before the giant comes back this way."

Mighty Eagle clapped his hands loudly letting the men know to redouble their efforts. "Hurry, warriors! He will be upon us soon. The fire must be hot!"

For the plan to work, they would have to slow the beast down, and then trap him in the cave while it was burning. If that failed, their back up plan was the military, but they were still twenty minutes out.

≫≫ ≪≪

Tamir-Benob managed to stand up. He was in a lot of pain. The weapon had caused internal injuries and several broken bones. Multiple ribs felt broken, and it was difficult for him to take a full breath. When he walked, a sharp pain shot up his entire rib cage. He had not felt pain like this in a long time. Normally he would need to rest for a day or two to recover from an injury this severe, but his rage was propelling him forward.

"Ironhorse, your plan did not work! I am still here," he shouted. He quickly ran up to the where Ironhorse had been standing before the blast. There was a trail and tracks leading back into another cavern. His night vision allowed him to see their tracks in the dirt. They must be trying to escape through a back entrance.

He lumbered into the side room. Their scent was here, but the humans were not. There was a small exit at the end of the cavern. He worked his way in, but there were rocks in front of the exit; the path was blocked. Unsure if Ironhorse had caused this blockage, Tamir-Benob decided that it would take too long to dig through. He needed to find another way out.

Tamir-Benob moved slowly out of the room looking for other exists. He heard noise at the other end of the cave. Other men were here, but he was not sure what they were doing. He looked around. He was in the cavern where the soldier had injured him. A piece of the anti-tank missile had careened off his body and hit the wall. The explosion had knocked away a portion of the rock and revealed where an entryway had been covered up. It was worth exploring before heading to the front of the cave, as it might be an exit

Using his shoulder, he pushed hard and knocked more of the remaining rock away to expose an opening. The force caused rocks to fall around him, and finally a passage opened into another room. It looked more like a ceremonial or burial room. Facing him was a rock table with several parchments, like what he had used to report on his life events.

Odd, this is a familiar parchment style, he thought. On the cave wall there was writing in his ancient language and paintings of battles with tribesman. He picked up a parchment and his heartbeat faster. It was an old scroll, made of vellum similar to what he had used a long time ago. He opened one and studied the language of his own tongue.

*After many battles with the Saxons in Britannia, and the rise of Ambrosius Aurelianus from the tribe of the Pendragon, our clan sailed across the great sea of darkness. The journey lasted a month's time, and we lost a few brothers on the trip. The new land near the shore was strange, but with much game and few men. The first men we met were in tribes and close to nature. These clans moved around the lands and fought bravely, although we conquered them and took their crops. They saw us as deities and were afraid of our might. This time was free of the Hebrew God and his followers.*

*Over time we met travelers who came from the seas and were red-haired Norseman. Their chief Erik fought with ferocity but was no match for our kind. They brought steel with them, and many warriors died on both sides. Later sailors from foreign lands near our homeland arrived. They spoke of the Hebrew God and the feats of the Nazarene. It became more difficult to exist without constant battle and bloodshed. After many years in the sea facing lands, we migrated to this land with mountains, fresh water, and large game. Along the way we conquered many tribes, taking their women. Our children were very tall and became great chieftains.*

He picked up another parchment and read.

*The new tribesman killed another one of our brothers. Their kind are smart and move with stealth. Their weapons are made with flint, with bows and arrows, and some have firesticks. They overwhelm us with large numbers, as we kill a hundred of their warriors for every one of our kind. Their warriors do not fear death. Our kind are few, and it may be time to head back across the great sea and rejoin our brothers and sisters in our homeland. Our kind lives for battle, but with so few of us, I fear we will cease to exist. We will decide our course after the winter passes. A few of our brothers have left and pursued adventure in other parts of this vast land toward the West.*

Tamir-Benob put down the scroll with regret, realizing he would not find any of his kind here. Ironhorse's people must have killed the last of his brothers and sisters. He would return the favor for his people tenfold. He turned to see the writing and pictures on the wall. They were images of battles with the tribesman. The last was a warning, stating his kind should leave, that the land of the eagles was cursed, and the people here were strong and may be too proud to conquer.

Tamir-Benob reflected on the warning and thought of the difficulty ahead. Lying next to the parchments was a large sword of fine steel. He picked it up and turned to walk out of the burial room with renewed determination. It would be faster to go back through the front entrance, although that meant killing the men there now. He wanted vengeance against the soldier who had caused him such pain a few minutes ago.

⤜⟫⟫⟫ ⟪⟪⟪⤛

Mighty Eagle gave the order to start lighting the logs in the entrance of the cave. They built their fire past the opening, but not close enough to have a chance meeting with the giant. The mini fires roared to a start. The men placed more logs to try and increase the size and temperature of the blaze. Several others, including Stone, stood near the base of the fire watching for the giant. He had his anti-tank missile reloaded in case the big man showed up.

Jim Blackhawk turned to Stone. "What is he up to?"

"Not sure. He's probably looking for an exit. But Whitman should have forced him to come back here. Let's hope the fire and smoke bother him like a normal man."

Mighty Eagle walked over to the men. "I think we need to send someone back to see if the creature is still there," he said.

218

Mighty Eagle said a silent prayer to the Great Spirit and walked over to his men. They knew what he was about to ask. Everyone understood that it was the best strategy, but it would likely be a death sentence for whoever went back. Two young warriors stepped forward to volunteer. Before the warriors could speak, Stone, who was still wearing night vision goggles, yelled, "I have movement coming this way. Everyone take cover. Incoming fast!"

"Get ready to fire!" yelled Jim Blackhawk as members of IA took their positions. They tried to block the impending exit of the giant through any seams near the fire logs.

As Tamir-Benob made his way toward the front of the cave, the smoke and heat grew stronger. Daylight popped through the haze. The warriors had caught him— probably descendants of the tribe who killed his ancient brothers. He saw two sizeable boulders with green moss nearby and prepared to launch them at the fire to create a hole to exit.

Many in the group now saw the beast for the first time. They were shocked at his size and muscularity. His red hair hung to his shoulders, his eyes shined orange around black irises, and his canine incisors were frightening. The resemblance to the demigods of Crow legends was uncanny. The giant heaved the stone like a missile at one of the walls of fire, knocking a large hole in it.

Stone screamed, "Fire! Fire now! Give it everything you got!"

The group raised their weapons and began to shoot. A volley of bullets went into the cave, and between the smoke and heavy amounts of musty gunpowder, the giant was momentarily lost to sight. A bellow from behind their view was unlike any they had ever heard; one that sounded like pain and rage tangled together.

Tamir-Benob, already hurt by the earlier battle in the cave, dropped to a knee. More pain, and such tenacity by this group. Blood trickled down his face and body. To slow the shots, he lobbed more large rocks above the fire and out toward the men, then hid behind a boulder to provide a momentary reprieve from the onslaught. The rocks he tossed managed to hit and injure a couple of men severely, further depleting their ranks. From behind his makeshift shield, the giant caught his breath and gathered another pile of rocks to use as missiles against the fire wall and the soldiers.

"Move over there and fill those holes with new wood," ordered Jim Blackhawk in an effort to keep the giant pinned down by the blaze. The fire roared loudly, and blue flames leapt up to ten feet in the sky. The temperature was intense.

Tamir-Benob was becoming more affected by the low oxygen and heat. He started to retreat to the rear of the cave. Stone jumped into action and fired his anti-tank rocket toward the Nephilim, but Tamir-Benob moved at the last moment and the missile hit the rock near him instead. There was a loud explosion. The impact disoriented the beast, but not for long. He gave Stone a long hard look through the flames as one swearing vengeance. His figure cast a large silhouette over the smoke and fire. With a final glance at the men and a shaking of his fist, he started back into the cave.

❧❧❧ ❦❦❦

Whitman and Ryan continued to make their way further from the cave.

"This way will take us back toward the military. It's a couple hours' hike but probably the safest way and puts distance from Tamir-Benob," Whitman assured her.

"Do you think Stone and the others can hold him off until the military arrives?"

"I do, but only if they keep the fire hot and push him back with their rifles. Let's just hope he doesn't decide to dig his way out the back."

"What are the chances of him making his way through the rubble at the back exit?"

"Small. We collapsed the walkway, but there's always the chance he could find his way through, especially if he gets desperate. Even more reason to keep moving fast. We won't see him if he's coming from behind us."

The thought of being chased gave Ryan shivers. She wouldn't put anything past that evil beast.

Whitman had lost contact with the team; they were most likely still battling Tamir-Benob inside the cave he told himself silently.

⋘⋙

Tamir-Benob moved back into the cave. The rest and recovery he wanted would have to wait. He was still having trouble breathing and would need to dig his way out. The sword would help to move the rubble.

As the giant disappeared further into the smoke, Mighty Eagle approached the group once more. "We need to go in, or we run the risk of him escaping."

"I'm going with you, Mighty Eagle," Stone interjected.

Mighty Eagle agreed, and the duo entered the cave around the edges of the fire along with two Crow tribesman. They left the others to stand guard. The group moved with determination as they tried to catch up with the big figure ahead of them.

⋘⋙

Whitman and Ryan were making slow, steady progress. They had heard shots in the distance at the cave, indicating a firefight with the creature. Still not being able to contact the group was worrisome, although Whitman had been in touch with the military. Two helicopters with troops should be arriving in the next few minutes to provide reinforcements. Even though they had made it out of the cave, Whitman still felt like there was not enough distance between them and Tamir-Benob to slow down.

Ryan was exhausted and needed frequent rest and hydration breaks.

The giant made his way to the back exit of the cave in the side cavern. Like a machine, he tunneled his way through the rubble near the collapsed ceiling. The old sword helped him dig, and he was able to push the rocks aside much quicker than a normal man could. Others were approaching, so he turned to face them.

Seeing the hybrid up close and at his full height frightened the advancing men. Mighty Eagle stopped in shock. He gripped his rifle and prepared to fire. The giant's teeth showed in his flashlight. Stone fired a couple quick rounds with his assault rifle and knocked the beast back. He disappeared into the shadows. How could he be injured and still move so fast?

A voice spoke from the shadows. "You men have come to your death. Your weapons will only slow me. I am old, and strong. Before your ancestors saw the first white man, I walked the land. There are writings here that showed my kind ruled this land and killed hundreds of your people. Prayer to your gods will not save you. I am the grandson of a spirit son of the Creator and move as the wind."

Then out of the darkness the giant was upon them. The nearest tribesman lost his head to the giant's sword. Tamir-Benob quickly grabbed the second young Crow and threw him across the room against the wall, snapping his neck. There was a horrible sound as the body slumped to the ground.

Only Stone and Mighty Eagle were left. As the giant approached Stone, he swung the butt of his rifle around and hit the creature in the head hard, drawing blood. They wrestled and Tamir-Benob pulled the gun away from the soldier. Stone grabbed his tactical knife and stabbed the giant in the leg, causing him to howl in pain and swing angrily at Stone. He ducked but was not quick enough, and the giant hit his shoulder. The pain was excruciating. Stone kicked at the giant's knee, but it felt more like hitting something akin to a block of cement. The giant picked Stone up by the neck. They were now staring at each other eye-to-eye. Tamir-Benob leaned over and took a bite of flesh out of Stone's shoulder. He yelled in agony and kicked for the giant's groin but only managed to connect with his abdomen.

"Time for you to die. Your effort was for nothing. My kind will return!" With that, Tamir-Benob tossed Stone against the jagged wall. With blood dripping from his nose, Stone looked over at the giant, raised a hand and pointed, and then slumped to the ground dead.

Mighty Eagle stood in shock as he faced the abomination. He pointed his rifle at the giant.

"Old man, you are an elder of the tribe. One with your spirit gods. Why do you think you can stand against me, something of legend?" Tamir-Benob matter of fact stated.

"You are an evil, a scourge from the old days, something that does not belong in our time. Legends describe how your people's actions brought the wrath of the Great One. My people destroyed your brothers before, and I will destroy you now." A defiant Might Eagle said.

"Do you think if your soldiers and kinsman could not stop me, that you can?"

"If you make it past me, Ironhorse will kill you. He has had visions of your confrontation. The spirits have foretold this and are with him."

"None of your spirits will help you now." Tamir-Benob quickly approached the tribal elder, but Mighty Eagle fired, grazing the giant's shoulder. Blood trickled down as Tamir-Benob knocked the rifle out of Mighty Eagle's hand. Mighty Eagle drew his large hunting knife and prepared for hand-to-hand combat. The Crow medicine man held his ground as the giant approached him.

The giant looked down on the determined man. "You can go now, and I will let you live. Or you can stay and die, elder."

"I would rather die a warrior's death than allow your kind to roam the earth." Mighty Eagle lunged forward with his knife but was a moment too slow. He overreached and the giant caught his arm midair. Tamir-Benob grabbed the knife and threw him back several feet.

He dropped the knife on the ground and walked menacingly toward Mighty Eagle. "Do you think your spirits will save you now? Wood spirits can do little against a fallen and his offspring.

Only the God of the Hebrew people can stop me. You do not pray to him."

"I don't need the gods to save me, only this." Mighty Eagle drew a throwing axe and hurled it at the giant. Unfortunately for the tribal elder, the giant caught the throw in midair—an inhuman grab. He tossed it to the ground. Mighty Eagle was frantic. As a last resort, he took out a small silver dagger and attempted to stab the giant as he walked closer. Tamir-Benob grabbed Mighty Eagle's hand and clamped down on his wrist until he dropped the dagger. While still in the giant's crushing grasp, Mighty Eagle reached up with his other hand and gouged his enemy in the eyes, momentarily stunning him. With a howl, Tamir-Benob released his Crow opponent.

Mighty Eagle thought of one last plan. If he could lure the Nephilim out of the cavern, and then push him over the edge of the walkway, the drop could possibly kill the beast.

"Your cowardly kindred were no match for my people," Mighty Eagle taunted. "Why do you think we destroyed your kind? In these very mountains hundreds of years ago, we burned alive the last of the giants."

Mighty Eagle slowly walked out of the cavern room, and the angry giant chased after him.

"Your insults only hasten your death," Tamir-Benob replied.

Mighty Eagle waited on the ledge of the walkway, overlooking a twenty-foot or more drop. As the giant approached, Mighty Eagle attempted to circle around and push him off, but the giant saw his plan and picked him up by his shirt. His feet dangled in the air several feet above the ground.

"You really thought you could trick me, elder?"

Mighty Eagle made one final effort and punched toward the giant's neck but missed. He was exhausted, and out of tricks. The creature's breath was hot and smelt like death.

Tamir-Benob held the tribal leader close, looking into his eyes. Mighty Eagle noted no spark of life in the giant, no compassion, only cold emptiness devoid of soul. The giant turned and walked toward the edge of the overhang.

Mighty Eagle closed his eyes and mouthed a small prayer.

"Your gods can take you now," Tamir-Benob said and then threw him over the ledge.

Mighty Eagle fell over twenty feet before hitting the ground with a thud. Many of his bones were broken in the fall, but Mighty Eagle crawled a few feet before looking up and breathing his last breath.

Without looking back, the giant picked up an automatic weapon and a knife and left to resume his digging. Time to find Ironhorse and end this.

# Chapter Twenty

# Bavaria Germany

**M**ULLINS WAS MEETING WITH the Chancellor for the first time. The Chancellor had flown in specifically to meet with him. After much discussion around technical aspects of their work, timelines, and needed resources, Mullins decided to inquire more about his benefactor.

"Chancellor, may I ask you questions of a more personal measure?"

"Yes, by all means Stephen, go ahead."

"What is your personal interest in the Nephilim, and what led to this work by your organization?"

"I, like several of the families involved with the council, have a deep rich history in Europe, going back in some cases a thousand or more years in our lineage. My family has stories in our archives of these creatures, including ancestors serving in the Order of the Temple of Solomon, or Knights Templar as many know them.

This history allowed us insight of how these beings ruled over the earth for several years. They were vicious and without mercy. A few relics have been preserved from this time.

"Just in the last few hundred years, work at the Vatican, the Eastern Orthodox Church in Istanbul, and the Coptic Churches of Ethiopia have provided separate insight on what you work on now. They have had members working in secret over the years to uncover and track these creatures, fearful of prophecy. We have watched closely, and even at times have had temporary working relationships.

"Years ago, these sources became convinced that the spiritual world would insert a much greater influence in the physical world in the end times. We believe that the time is rapidly approaching for their return. Most in this world will be caught unaware and become casualties of the arriving apocalypse. The council wants to meet the aggressors on a level playing field," the Chancellor explained.

"My own research suggests that in the end times the Nephilim and fallen will come back to earth, in preparation of a greater battle, like in the days of the biblical Noah. I now better understand what that means," commented Mullins.

"Yes, part of the reason we recruited you was for your beliefs and openness to what sounds like a fairy tale. If man only understood that what we now call supernatural was commonplace on this earth thousands of years ago.

"The Vatican, and several other groups around the world, are terrified of this happening and are working to prepare for it.

Until now, no one had any insight at how much destruction these creatures could bring. Think, if the best military in the world lost fifty soldiers fighting one of these beasts, what destruction would one hundred or a thousand of these hybrids bring?

"We think one of the best ways to prepare is through augmentation of our own biology so we can align with, or at least be able to defend ourselves against, these monstrosities."

"How convincing is your proof?" Mullins asked.

"We will share that with you in good time, but the authenticity is above reproach and from many secret sources and societies. We have our own archives and librarian, including documents from early Christian and Jewish leaders that are over two thousand years old. There are secret supplemental writings of the book of Enoch we have in our possession, as well as firsthand accounts from nonreligious leaders. The emperors of Rome were so fearful of remaining giants left in their lands that they had specialized teams to hunt them unbeknownst to most Roman citizens.

"But the best source material is held by religious sects, and in some instances European governments. There are also other government groups, such as your military, researching along these lines, but none who have a living Nephilim within their grasp. From what you tell us, it is doubtful that the American military can control the current creature."

"That's true. Unless they completely destroy much of his body, I doubt they will be able to capture and contain him.

Perhaps if he were given a high dosage of anesthetics, but the hard part is to contain him long enough to do that. His body seemed to adapt to the drugs we used, and over time higher dosages were required to control him. When do you think, they will return to our world?"

"There is no way to know for sure, at least with the information left behind. But we all see world events growing worse. Some of the documents suggest that instability in the world, famine, and more environmental calamities will preclude their return. Most likely there will be isolated incidents of Nephilim at first in varying parts of the world. We are seeing that now, and there are reports of possibly others several miles away where this one was captured," the Chancellor noted.

"Beyond the genetics work, what other preparations are being made?" Mullins asked.

"We have self-contained bunkers that allow energy production and food growth hidden away if that need ever arises. There is also a small group of council military forces training to protect our people in the event of a return. Of course, against creatures such as this, there is no guarantee how long before they would find us. I doubt any army in this world could last very long against an onslaught such as that.

"The ideal situation would be to use the work you are leading to transform ourselves into stronger, smarter, and longer-living beings. This will allow us to centralize even more influence and control. Once that is in place, and assuming the fallen and their children return, we will be a more formidable force they have to deal with.

"I am a realist and doubt we will completely be at their level, but perhaps we will be strong enough to give them pause. Faced with human hybrids who can compete with them, they may have little choice but to allow some accommodations. It will be hard enough to control billions of people, let alone a small group of super men and women. If the prophecies are true, they will only have so much time before they will need to deal with the angels of God also."

"So better for this group to rule in hell on earth than serve in heaven?" Mullins asked.

"Milton was partially correct. I see this as taking control of our destiny. None of us are interested in bowing down to creatures who kill without purpose or for sport. My suspicion is they only recognize strength and raw power. This is our best way to protect our kind from permanent servant hood."

"Is there any source material I can study? Besides an interest, I would like to learn more about the history of these creatures if possible."

"Yes, I will ask the archivist to share some reading material with you to get started. Over time we will share more with you."

Mullins left feeling confident about his decision to leave the army and focus on a more impactful endeavor.

Later that evening, Mullins enjoyed a walk near the lake. A partial moon brightly reflecting on the water gave the area a serene, calming look—his own Eden. A calm before the storm. He reflected on what was probably transpiring in the United States. Ryan was most likely dead, Stone as well. He was a good soldier, and Mullins had a small bit of remorse over Stone's death. General Briggs would have called in heavy artillery to control the beast. The IA agent, Whitman, would have been the most curious and was likely tracking the hybrid and possibly confronting him.

By now the military had the DNA sample, and others would be brought in to determine how to weaponize their findings. He was months, if not years ahead of the Americans, but eventually they would experiment with soldiers. Surely the council realized that multiple competing groups would have Nephilim hybrid humans in the future. But perhaps that would increase humanities odds against the coming onslaught. But still so many unknowns.

A large bounty had likely been placed on his head and caution was necessary for survival, as unknown operatives would be searching for him. The clock was ticking, and eventually he would need to move to their other lab locations in the Middle East or Northern Africa to keep searchers off his tracks. Having a clone of Subject Alpha that was controllable might be of added benefit. The council's vast network was proactively watching for others and had contingencies in place. They had satellite jamming technology to prevent imagery of his movement, at least at the compound.

The verdict was out as to how long he would stay with the council, or if he would be better off on his own. At least until he could find a way to transfect the hybrid's genetic material into himself, he would continue this collaboration of convenience.

Gunther was trailing Mullins as he walked by the lake. The council was putting their trust in this man. He wasn't convinced of Mullins's loyalty. He had experienced too many sheep in wolves clothing. A man who spent so much time with the US military, with some of its greatest secrets, and then to defect so quickly was a traitor in his mind. If he defected once, he would do it again. Van Wilhelm had asked him to discreetly watch Mullins, just as a precaution. If Mullins did anything disloyal to the council he would be there to stop him. So far Mullins had made the right decisions, but there was a long way to go.

Back in the United States, Briggs moved several pieces on the chess board. Once this mission was complete, he would put in his retirement papers and join the security firm, one of the largest with hands in every major war event across the globe. He had been building the relationship with the group for years.

With his contacts across the military complex, the creation of a consortium of power brokers with clout behind the scenes had been opportunistic. A unique collection of soldiers, greedy government agents, and pharmaceutical executives made up the group he was joining. They had influence even at the White House and it reminded him o an X-files group. One thing had remained constant with man over the years, his greed and willingness to do most anything to have more.

He had managed to limit the full extent of their findings with the Nephilim to US officials, so only a select few realized the true potential they held in their hands. He would use this opportunity to expand his new group's power base and influence. Slowly under his influence, the consotium would create the perfect soldier for hire and then offer the technology to world leaders. What price would a third world country pay for the abilities of a Nephilim?

Mullins was an unexpected wrinkle, but his contractors from the CIA world would find and neutralize him.

# Chapter Twenty-One

# The End is Near

RYAN AND WHITMAN STOPPED for a break at a stream as they continued their escape from the giant. The military had finally arrived at the front of the cave to assist in the fight, but because of their remote location, a pickup for the duo was out of the question. So, they would continue on toward a rendezvous at the military's location, hopeful they were not being followed.

Ryan used the break to find out more about Whitman. "So, you were military before joining the IA?"

"Yea, I was young and felt a little lost. The army made sense. It taught me discipline and gave me direction."

"More than direction, you were in the Army Rangers, right? And did tours in the Middle East?"

"Yes, I was craving adventure. You do crazy things when you're young. There were some things over there— unexplainable things. Tracks of creatures that didn't belong, noises at night, and there were others who said they saw things in the dark. Some spooky stuff, but nothing like this."

"You were close to this creatures home, weren't you? Did you hear about giants back then?" Ryan asked.

"Not like this. I heard of mountain men, those who took children. They were described as wild uncivilized savages who stayed away from civilization. I saw tribesman while on patrol, but nothing that I would describe as nonhuman, although there were many places that could have hidden this creature. Anytime we ventured near the caves, it always felt like we were in another time. No one wanted to go very far into the caves, and only if we were scouting for Al Qaeda or the Taliban. I was glad to get back to the States and get on with the next chapter of my life."

"Why did you go into law enforcement? You could have made a lot more money in private security."

"Growing up, there wasn't a great deal of law and order on the reservation. The elders tried to police things, but it wasn't the same as having a real law enforcement presence to make people feel safe. My people are very suspicious to begin with, and they would rather have a Crow lead their police force than a nontribesman. I enjoy it—the helping people part—except when we deal with the occasional hard-core criminal."

"I definitely understand that. Are you married, or have children?"

"I'm widowed. My wife died a few years ago. But my teenage daughter keeps me busy," Whitman said.

"I'm sorry to hear that. I really didn't mean to pry. What's your daughter's name, if you don't mind me asking."

"That's ok. Her name is Katrina. She's the light of my life. What about you? Husband? Kids?" Whitman said, shifting the focus back to Ryan.

"My work has always been my life. Some days I think there's a void but being in the military and working in a secret lab doesn't lend itself to meeting people, if you know what I mean. I'm close with my mom and my brother, but that's about it. After medical school and a research fellowship, a life in the military called. Took ten years of hard work, and I thought we were doing the right thing until Mullins turned on us," Ryan said, turning her face away.

"What did Mullins do? I knew he was gone, but never heard what happened. He seemed like the typical military officer when we met."

"No one knows this, but when we were out trying to assist the army in the state park, the creature approached us. A couple of mercenaries showed up right before the giant. I guess they had been hunting him. At first, I thought they were going to shoot us, but apparently Mullins had made a deal with them, and when Subject Alpha approached, Mullins pushed me forward and offered me in a trade. When Tamir-Benob grabbed me, Mullins left with the mercenaries. That was right after Subject Alpha killed the US soldier who was with us."

"That's crazy. Mullins was a traitor. We knew he disappeared. His car was found abandoned later, but the army is still trying to find him. This entire situation is scary. With the knowledge Mullins has of the creature and the biology behind it, there are a lot of countries that would pay millions for him if he defected. I want to discuss this more, but we really need to keep moving," Whitman said, gathering up their belongings.

Ryan looked over at him. He seemed more human than warrior now. He had a strong rugged masculinity about him that she found that very appealing.

Tamir-Benob finished digging through the cave-in. It felt good to stand up in the daylight, out of the musty, smoke-filled cave. He caught the scent of the woman and the warrior Ironhorse. Finding them was his priority. Then he would head toward the mountain peak to escape those tracking him. He would look for sustenance along the way. Fatigue was setting in, but he would push through it. He took off, quicker than any human man could travel.

The two military helicopters hovered near the front of the cave, lowering just close enough to the ground for the highly trained Ranger team to descend. Normally active troops would not be deployed on US soil, but the president had given the go ahead. General Briggs had selected the team himself.

Captain Rodriguez, commander of the team, spoke to Jim Blackhawk with IA to assess the situation. Rodriguez was briefed by Briggs beforehand but was still in disbelief about the size and nature of the reported creature. This particular Ranger team had some previous experience with unusual situations, including being assigned to track cryptoid sightings. Rodriguez's motto was if they could track it, they could kill it. A second extraction team was on standby to take the body away at the end of the mission.

"First squad, enter the cave and send images back. We need to know what is going on."

The squad moved around the fire and entered the cave without speaking. They made their way to the back slowly, using night vision and lamps to light the cave. The trip was eerily silent. They reached the back of the cave where it went upward toward an entry way to another cavern. As the team moved forward at the base of steep walkway, the bloodied body of Mighty Eagle lay on the hard cave floor. The remainder of Whitman's team saw the image on Rodriguez's camera screen. All went silent, somber at the death of their tribal leader.

"Damn that thing," cursed an angry Jim Blackhawk.

The Ranger team continued up and to the back of the alcove near the walkway where they found Stone's bruised and broken body against a wall. It looked like he had been in a struggle. Two other dead tribesmen lay nearby. A massacre. The soldiers continued further and found a passage that led unobstructed out the cave.

"The crazy beast has gone after Ironhorse and Dr. Ryan. We have to warn them," Jim Blackhawk warned ominously.

Rodriguez started to give orders. "Let's call in air support to search for them. Our men will go on foot to intercept the creature."

The remaining military team members stayed to take the bodies out of the cave, except Jim Blackhawk, who left with the Ranger team to intercept Tamir-Benob.

⟫⟫⟫ ⟪⟪⟪

Tamir-Benob was making fast time, and he was catching up with Ironhorse and Ryan. He had come across a wild boar along the way, devoured the meat raw, and then quickly washed off in a stream before continuing on his way. The sustenance gave him strength, and his body started to heal. His recent kill had allowed the acquisition of a knife and gun, and he still had the sword from the interior room in the cave. He should be able to use the firestick if needed. It was growing cloudy and looked like a storm was coming. The rain would make it harder for the others to track him. He smiled as a drop of rain fell on his cheek. He would have the advantage.

⟫⟫⟫ ⟪⟪⟪

Whitman had just gotten off the phone with Jim Blackhawk and had learned about Stone and Mighty Eagle. It wasn't a good time to break the news to Ryan. Their deaths would not be in vain. The brave men had bought them valuable time, but the giant was in fast pursuit. They were good men, and he would mourn them when this was all over.

Good that the Rangers were on the scene, but the helicopters could not land or get a clean shot with the thick dense forest. The trees were tight around Whitman and Ryan as well, blocking out a lot of light and making it difficult to keep a fast pace. Every shadow looked like the giant. It was another couple miles to get back to the cave where they could meet the soldiers on foot, and they would most likely be caught before then.

"Where do things stand?" Ryan asked.

"Good and bad news. The good news is the Ranger team arrived. They have boots on the ground and are making their way toward us to escort us in. Helicopters are overhead as well, but they don't have a clear site for landing. We have a few more miles to go, so will keep at it."

"And the bad news?" a weary Ryan asked.

"Bad news is that Tamir-Benob dug out of the cave where we exited. The Ranger team found no sign of him. It's possible he went elsewhere, but we all think he's tracking us."

"That's not just bad news, that's horrible news. He clearly has a hatred for you and is obsessed about finding us. Why is that?"

"My people's legends suggest we fought some of his kind hundreds of years ago. The battle lasted for many, many years. They killed hundreds of our people, and our stories suggests we wiped out the last of their kind in a cave with a fire. We tried to replicate that set up when he came in the cave after us."

"Just great. Yeah, he mentioned some of that history. He said that you reminded him of earlier warriors he fought. He almost seemed afraid of you. If your people fought his people, and you reminded him of a long-ago strong warrior, he may feel compelled to seek you out."

"We need to assume he's coming. He'll probably catch us before we can get more help. We need to find a defensible position."

"Where would that be?" Ryan asked.

"Either a hill or cave with strategic barriers. None of that is ideal. But if we can at least see him coming that gives us a better chance. There should be a place in the next mile we can use as base camp. Hopefully that will give us enough time to allow the military to join the fight."

Ryan sighed. This was going to be a long tough day.

The Ranger squad was leveraging Jim Blackhawk's expertise to track the creature. They exited the back of the cave and tried to make up the distance. The second squad started out in front of the cave working their way toward Whitman. They were at least one to two hours from reaching him because of the terrain, and they weren't optimistic they could reach him before the giant did.

⇢⇢⟩⟩ ⟨⟨⟨⟵

Tamir-Benob knew he was getting close to Ironhorse. He had picked up a long stick and sharpened it while he walked. He was heavily armed and would catch them momentarily. Although a little fearful, he would enjoy this kill. He had not known such frustration, pain, and anger in over a thousand years. His body was getting stronger the more time he had to heal.

⇢⇢⟩⟩ ⟨⟨⟨⟵

Whitman noted a cave on a hill as they made their way through the forest. There was still lots of foliage near them, but maybe it would be enough room for an airlift. If not, they would at least have some visibility to see the approaching giant.

"Given the circumstances, are we better off trying to go faster and meet the Ranger team?" Ryan asked.

"I don't think so. Based on our last communication, he'll catch us before we reach them. Then we'll have the problem of him cornering us in a defenseless position. At least here we can see him coming. Another problem, the clouds are coming fast. We're going to get rain shortly. It would be a nightmare to be in the open when he attacks. If by a small chance he's not tracking us, we'll stay dry and meet the military here in a bit."

"I would really prefer not to see him again. None of these ideas are good." Ryan shook her head and looked out in the direction they came from for a few seconds.

"I'd feel a little better if you gave me a gun," she said.

"Sure," Whitman agreed and handed her his Glock.

She shoved it in her waistband, and they continued walking to the base of the cave mouth. The cave itself was small, and a few bats flew out as they entered. Ryan shuddered as the creepy black winged creatures flew by.

Whitman quickly set up a makeshift base behind a large boulder. "We don't have large armaments, so we have to be able to find a way to stun him. I think the only way to stop him is to take his head like when David slew Goliath. Fortunately, Mighty Eagle kept this tomahawk razor-sharp."

"Is that enough?

"I don't know, but it's probably our best chance."

"Let me say one thing, then?"

"Sure."

"I appreciate you coming back to save me. I don't know if we'll make it out of here. But if we do, I'd like to grab dinner and have a nice glass of wine if you're interested."

Whitman let out a soft laugh and shook his head. "Sounds good to me, Kathryn. Let's just make sure we get out of here. I could really go for some Italian food with a glass of Chianti."

Ryan smiled at that—the first normal conversation in over two days. She was proud of herself, asking out a super attractive guy, even though she had not showered, her hair was a mess, and she wasn't wearing a stitch of makeup.

Whitman prepared a couple of sharp spears, although he wasn't super optimistic about their chances. His phone rang. He jumped, surprised that he had any connection here. "That was Rodriguez, the Army team lead. They are making progress, but its slow going. The helicopter is heading our direction, but storm clouds and mountains are slowing them down. We're on our own for a bit."

Ryan wanted to scream but wasn't going to let the creature get the best of her. As she looked out of the cave, the dark clouds rolled in. Lightning crackled in the distance. She could only imagine the giant watching them now. How could things get any worse?

⇾⇉⇉ ⇇⇇⇇

The Ranger squad tracked in silence. Jim Blackhawk saw signs of the giant. They were having trouble making up ground. The team had never tracked anything that could move through the forest this quick. They were fearful they would be too late. A light rain began to fall. They put on their ponchos and moved forward somberly in the dreadful conditions.

## Chapter Twenty-Two
# Final Confrontation

**W**HITMAN USED A FEW minutes to explore the cave. The entrance went less than a quarter mile back. With no exit in the back, they would have to go through Tamir-Benob to escape. He went to work building a trap for the fiend.

"If we aren't able to stop him outside the cave, we can use this punji pit as a fail-safe, but we'll have to lure him over here."

"I hope we don't have to use it, but it looks lethal. It'll definitely slow him down," Ryan said, staring into the pit at the jagged spears.

Their flashlights were still working, but he was fearful how long their batteries would hold out.

Now it was a waiting game. Who would catch up with them first, their allies or a blood thirsty savage bent on killing them and possibly eating them. They positioned themselves out of view if the giant entered the cave.

"Do you really believe his story about being a product of angel and man?" Ryan asked.

"I do now. Growing up we were told stories that mirrored creatures like him. Other cultures have comparable legends, and a lot of these tales have a small bit of truth. My tribe has other superstitions focused on skin-walkers and Sasquatch, so who knows? I've spent a lifetime in the forest, and most of the things I saw were explainable until I went to the Middle East, and now this."

"My life was quite different than yours. I grew up in the city, attended private school, and was never exposed to the outdoors until the military. Even then it was always with lots of other soldiers or in a lab environment. There were never any discussions around nonhuman entities. Things began to change the last few years. Leadership in the military became more open-minded about using enhanced humans and looking for other ways to augment soldier performance. Right before this started, I began to hear rumors about nonhumans. Some of the stories were not believable, but it makes me think someone higher up was aware of these creatures before now. Mullins seemed aware, but I didn't think it was odd at the time."

"That's usually the case. Soldiers like us aren't told until decisions are made, and we're there to execute orders, not give our opinion. Do you think General Briggs knew?"

"Possibly, but I suspect it goes higher than him. He's old-school military; he was very leery of biological enhancements when I initially met him."

"Yea, this smells like CIA or even a Department of Defense Black Ops program. It's unusual that a special operations team is here. They normally don't set foot on US soil with direct action missions unless there is something going on the public was not supposed to hear about."

"Do you think that means we're expendable?"

Whitman paused a minute. "I hope not. But with so many deaths, what are a few more at this point? Put a bullet in our heads, add a cover story. Who would know? It depends on how much of a risk we're perceived as," Whitman rationalized.

As they continued to talk, Tamir-Benob was approaching a small opening at the base of a hill near the cave where Whitman and Ryan hid. The light rain dripped down his back. He had tied his hair in a ponytail to keep it from blowing into his face.

Their scent was strong. They were waiting for him in the small cave ahead. The warrior would have chosen this location because of its defensive advantage.

Tamir-Benob stayed on the outer edge of the forest, watching, listening. He heard the faint sound of human voices inside amongst the thunder overhead. He grinned in anticipation. Finally, time to end this.

Whitman held his hand up to stop conversation. Although the storm had picked up, he was aware of activity outside the cave. His senses were on high alert.

"What is it? I don't see anything," Ryan whispered.

"Do you hear that? The forest is suddenly silent. It's not the storm, but the presence of a predator will do that. He's probably close."

"You can hear through the storm?" an amazed Ryan asked.

Whitman moved to the entrance of the cave, careful to shield himself from a thrown spear or rock attack by the giant. He gripped his Winchester close and noticed slight movement on the right side of the opening in front of the cave. Not much, just enough to move the bushes.

He spoke softly. "I see you; you can't hide from me." He would wait a little longer and let Tamir-Benob approach them and make the first move.

He turned to Ryan and whispered, "He's just beyond the bushes, about twenty-five meters away. Be very quiet and still." They had turned off their flashlights.

Ryan gulped and looked intensely ahead, waiting for the creature to step out.

Tamir-Benob threw a rock to the opposite side of the cave entrance, which made a large crash when it landed. Whitman signaled to Ryan to stay in place. The giant was trying to goad them into making a move. If Whitman had not been watching closely, he might have been tempted to step out and gauge the nature of the disturbance.

After another sixty seconds or so the giant stepped out of the clearing in the rain facing the cave. Lightning lit up his silhouette amongst the trees, and he spoke loudly. "Ironhorse, I know you and the woman are inside. Show yourself. I challenge you to come out and face me!"

The giant began to walk forward toward Whitman, carrying a spear and a gun. He had a sword and knife in his belt. Whitman realized the gun the beast was carrying was Stone's. Whitman stood up slowly and walked to the edge of the cave to face the giant. The wind picked up as he moved forward. His gait was slow and deliberate, showing no fear. Ryan looked on horrified.

He pointed his Winchester at the giant. "That is far enough. You could surrender, and the military probably wouldn't even kill you."

Tamir-Benob put down his spear and stolen firestick and turned to speak directly to Whitman. His appearance elicited fear, which Whitman fought to contain.

"Ironhorse, you are the only one worthy to fight me. Do you think I would ever surrender? No, we are going to fight like warriors of old to the death. That is my way. After your death I will take your woman, and then create more of my kind."

"You aren't going to do any of that, beast. I'm not going to let you leave here. Our people are resilient and stronger than you think."

"There are others of my kind still left in this world, and many, many more waiting for the right vessels to return. The strongest of my kind maintain their consciousness at death nearby, waiting and watching. What do you think will happen when your doctors try to replicate men like me? Strong empty vessels will allow the crossing over of my kind."

"You talk too much, beast."

"Only so you know what will happen after you die. The first of my kind before the great flood were bigger and stronger than me. Their fathers, the fallen, still wait to return to this world to avenge their earlier defeat. The same mistake will not be made again. We will dominate man and rule with no mercy or alliances. Man will submit and serve or will be exterminated."

Ryan walked to the side of the cave as she could take no more. If the giant was correct, they were creating the perfect environment for more of these creatures to return.

Whitman frowned as rain dripped down his forehead. "You overestimate your importance, beast. Man has grown too powerful since your kind ruled. Our weapons will cut you down. If not man, the Creator will send another event to destroy you. Your overconfidence and pride will be your kind's downfall."

Ryan interjected herself. She would go down fighting. She walked back to face the creature with the Glock pointed at him. "Tamir-Benob, if you have this much fight from us, what do you expect from billions of people?"

"Woman, you have conviction, but that will not save you. My kind were created to rule, and your people are weak, easily ruled, like sheep. You can shoot me, and it will do little damage. Ironhorse, come closer and fight me or I will come up there."

Whitman had sent a message to the Ranger team a minute ago, but they were at least another ten to fifteen minutes out at best. He stepped out from the cave entrance to approach the giant.

Ryan shouted, "Frank, stop!"

"Kathryn, it'll be ok. Remember what we discussed earlier about punji's."

She immediately realized the dangerous plan he was considering.

Tamir-Benob smiled as the Crow warrior stepped out to face him. The giant towered over Whitman by several feet.

Whitman quickly fired off two rounds with his Winchester, striking the giant center mass and knocking him back several feet. Wanting to press his advantage, Whitman sprinted forward and used his reinforced tomahawk to chop at the giant.

Tamir-Benob dodged at the last second and the blade only hit his shoulder, but it caused a large gash. He howled and swung wildly but missed. Whitman quickly landed a kick to the creature's knee that knocked him off balance.

Tamir-Benob looked up, bracing himself. "Not bad, warrior, but now it is my turn." He backhanded Whitman with such force that he skidded across the dirt. "Ah, you do bleed."

Whitman wiped the blood off his lip. The blow had hurt, but he had rolled at the last second and minimized the impact. He jumped to his feet and circled the giant before slowly pulling his knife, taking in the sound of blade against leather. Determination spread across his face. The giant lunged forward, but Whitman side-stepped and stabbed Tamir-Benob in the leg. A vital spot was hit, and blood poured down the beast's side.

"You will have to do better than that," Tamir-Benob said, pushing Whitman hard. Whitman landed hard against a rock and felt a piercing pain in his ribcage.

Tamir-Benob pulled his sword and limped menacingly toward Whitman.

"No, you don't get to do that you bastard," Ryan yelled, distracting the giant momentarily. She ran toward them, pulled the Glock, and fired three quick shots. The Nephilim fell into the mud, more surprised than hurt by the bullets. Ryan helped Whitman up and they shuffled back to the entrance of the cave.

"We have to keep him back a few more minutes. The others will be here to help soon." Whitman said. Ryan nodded as they continued their retreat back into the cave.

The giant let out a howl that sound more like an animal than a human. "You can't escape me. I am coming for you both."

⤙⤚

Jim Blackhawk and the Ranger squad were approaching fast. The rain had made it more difficult, but they were ready to engage. Too many casualties, too many dead friends because of this creature. Frank was like a brother, believed in Jim when maybe others would not. He had to get there in time to help.

They heard the gunshots as they came into a clearing. No one was in sight, and their target was most likely in the cave ahead. The team stopped to assess next steps.

"We need to go now, Captain," Jim Blackhawk said trying to push the group ahead.

"I need to report to military command before we go into the cave," Rodriguez said. He was anxious to go in too, but there were protocols that must be followed.

"That'll cost us precious time. That thing could be killing Whitman and Dr. Ryan right now."

"Give me thirty seconds and we'll go in," assured Rodriguez.

The team waited for him to send a mission update to central command, but something felt off.

Jim Blackhawk had been on combat missions in the past, and this smelled fishy. He rechecked his rifle once again. Tension was knotting up in his shoulders. Second squad was still an hour away, so they would do this with half of the initial Ranger team.

The clouds had turned black, and lightning began to rage above them. Thunder rumbled ominously all around them. The storm was moving fast across the mountains. The dark sky cut out any light that would be in the cave. The rain was intensifying. Rodriguez finished his update with the general and signaled the team to move forward.

Whitman and Ryan made it back further in the cave. They heard Tamir-Benob coming behind them as they made their way toward the punji pit. The beast was running at them in a full gait and was closing in fast when he suddenly disappeared.

"What happened? He was close," Ryan said.

"I don't know. He may have ducked behind those boulders to see what we're doing. Stay here. He's trying to lure us out," Whitman cautioned.

Tamir-Benob circled back, sensing others in the fight. He slowly made his way to the front of the cave using some of the rocks and boulder as cover. He counted ten men out front. If he took a few men out now that would give them pause before they came any further and allow him time to go back for Ironhorse. He would have to fight his way out, but he doubted their weapons could kill him. Picking up two spears, he moved toward the front of the cave.

Rodriguez felt uneasy. It was too quiet, and there was no movement whatsoever. The rain and fog were interfering with his night vision and heat sensors. The team advanced slowly with IA taking the rear. Jim Blackhawk had a bad feeling too. Everything in him was screaming *danger*.

Tamir-Benob stepped out of the darkness of the cave and launched his spears; each one hit a mark and two Rangers were now dead. He pulled out Stone's SCAR-H assault rifle and fumbled with the firing mechanism. His fingers were too big for these tiny human weapons.

"Pull back, pull back," yelled Rodriguez.

The men retreated out of the cave. They were all seasoned fighters, but the sheer size and ferocity of the giant shook them. As they retreated to a more defensible position behind several trees, Rodriguez assigned two men to stand guard and watch for movement in the cave.

"What was that thing?" Rodriguez asked Jim Blackhawk.

"The giant you were briefed on, the hybrid who is part spirit and part man. Christian mythology calls it a Nephilim, a product of angelic lineage with humans described in the bible in Genesis 6. An incredibly hard to kill creature that the military thought was a clever idea to bring here, endangering our people."

"Not sure if I believe all the religious stuff. We need to go back, but we have to lure it out. We can't fight that thing in the cave. There're too many places for it to hide."

"I'm going back in with or without you. Whitman and Ryan are still in there," exclaimed Jim Nighthawk.

"I'm with you, but we can't just walk in there. We're going to smoke him out. I have an idea."

Tamir-Benob started back toward Whitman, cornered between the two groups.

After hearing the skirmish, Whitman was on edge. "Be ready. He has to come back our way since the soldiers are blocking his exit."

If he could force the giant back out, they might have a chance at stopping him. Whitman heard the beast creeping toward them. His feet scraped the ground, and he walked with a slight limp, still recovering from earlier injuries. Whitman stepped out from behind his hiding place, startling the giant. He raised his rifle and fired.

Tamir-Benob fell to his knees and yelled in pain. "Fight me like a warrior of old, Ironhorse. Firesticks are reserved for dogs. You are not a coward like those in your military. Your heart beats strong, and your passion runs deep. We are alike. I challenge you to hand-to-hand combat."

Whitman held up his knife, the striated edges gleaming ever so slightly, and waved the giant forward. "We are nothing alike. You are a sadistic killer. Come to me, giant. Let me show you the steely tip of my blade. You may bigger and stronger, but I am a member of the proud Crow Tribe." Ironhorse wanted to take a defensive position but needed to goad the giant to approach him.

"Once I kill you, Ironhorse, the others will quickly fall, and I will take the woman to the mountain top. She will birth the first of my children. I will stay hidden in the hills and capture more woman of your proud tribe."

"That is *not* going to happen. I remind you again creature, you overestimate your ability."

"Do you think you can stop me?"

"You sound like Goliath bragging to David. And how did that turn out for you and your kind?"

Ryan could stomach no more and came out of her hiding place with the Glock pointed directly at Tamir-Benob.

"So, the woman reappears. She has courage," goaded the giant.

"Enough courage to neuter you, you abomination!"

The giant ignored Ryan and slowly walked toward Whitman. He took one more step forward, but in the dark he missed the drop off, which was partially concealed with branch leaves, and fell into the pit. The fall was about ten feet, but there were wooden spikes waiting for him at the bottom. As he fell, bone and tissue ripped, sounding like wood splintering. For any normal man, this would have sheared through tendons, and likely would have caused wounds large enough to bleed out and die.

The beast roared in pain and was stuck. He didn't understand how he could be trapped like this. For just a moment he felt fear. If he couldn't free himself, Ironhorse could kill him. He struggled violently trying to break free and wailed in agony.

"What have you done to me? You dare try to trap me like this," the enraged beast yelled!

Ryan watched as Tamir-Benob clawed at the walls and shoveled dirt out violently.

His incredibly tough skin had protected his feet somewhat, but the spikes had penetrated his feet a half inch before collapsing under his weight. He looked up, vengeance in his eyes. No one had ever humiliated him like this before.

"Stop, Tamir-Benob. If you try to climb out, we will have to kill you," Whitman stated matter of factly.

"You will die for this treachery, Ironhorse. I am coming for you and the woman."

In one quick motion, he propelled himself out of the hole and to a standing position outside the pit. He was covered in blood and caked dirt and was nearly unrecognizable.

"Take some hot steal!" Ryan pulled the trigger and knocked him back before he could reach for Whitman.

Whitman also fired a shot with his rifle, knocking the giant down. He grabbed his tomahawk and swung it at the giant, who met the attack with his sword. Whitman reversed and hit at the giant again scoring a blow to the shoulder. Tamir-Benob bent over in pain as blood gushed from the wound. He swung around and backhanded Whitman in the side of the face, knocking him back against the wall.

Ryan had reloaded the Glock and fired again, hitting the giant in the upper torso. He stopped his attack on Whitman and look at her. His shoulder stung from the bullets.

"I am going to enjoy killing you later, woman."

"You can try all you want, but you've failed so far."

They could hear the noise of approaching soldiers, and chalky smoke was beginning to fill the cave, making it harder to breathe.

Tamir-Benob stepped forward before Whitman could recover and knocked the gun from Ryan's hand. He grabbed her forcibly and tossed her over his shoulder. He wasn't quite ready to give her up just yet. She would birth strong offspring, or at least be a nice temporary shield for his escape.

"Put me down you coward!" she screamed. She tried to fight him off to no avail.

Whitman tried to get up but was too slow to stop the giant. Faced with either fighting Ironhorse or the troops, Tamir-Benob turned and moved through the cave toward the advancing soldiers.

# Chapter Twenty-Three
# Last Stand

I N BETWEEN CALLS WITH Captain Rodriguez at the Montana cave, General Briggs spoke with an unnamed caller. Whittman, Ryan, Rodriguez, and the injured sniper boarded the helicopter, glad to finally be out of this nightmare.

"General, I received your message, where are things now?"

"Ranger team is closing in on the creature. There was a dust up with the local Indian Affairs agents and some Crow tribesman. But we have helicopters ready for the extraction when he is taken down. There is a good chance of at least recovering his body."

"Good, at this point we can assume more tissue harvest for DNA experimentation later," asked the unnamed caller.

"Yes. Having the body will accelerate our work. The military will take the body, but I will make sure our scientist from the special activities center will receive the additional tissue and samples from the creature."

"And the field team chasing the creature?"

"The creature went after the Indian Affairs agent. They're converging in the mountains on tribal land. Most of the team have died, and we'll probably lose a few more before this is over."

"Can you assure the survivors' cooperation?"

"Those in the military, yes. We are still working on the IA group."

"Good. Although if they did go public, who would believe that a three-thousand-year-old giant is running around killing people? Any word on Colonel Mullins?"

"Still AWOL. We have assets looking for him, but no luck yet. We have confirmation that an adversary was working with him to leave the country. We'll eventually find him, but we believe he helped with the original escape of the subject. I'm assuming he's continuing his work with a stolen sample."

"It is paramount that we develop this quicker than the others."

"Understood. Has the White House contact been briefed?"

"They will be updated later, after we clean this up."

"Good. Then the president will only be aware of what we tell him."

***

Near the cave where the battle was taking place, Rodriguez led his Ranger team back after the giant. They were using smoke grenades to flush him out. Hopefully, they could retrieve Whitman and Ryan, but it looked doubtful. Jim Blackhawk and other tribe members brought up the rear. The tribal leaders had been updated of the situation and were discussing options in the event the creature made it deeper into tribal territory.

Unbeknownst to the team, General Briggs had sent Switchblade 300 drones with missiles to target the beast if he escaped. This whole thing was becoming a PR disaster for the government, and at this point they would track the giant's location with satellite imagery and take him down at all costs.

Rodriguez and his team had intercepted the giant and Dr. Ryan. He gave a hand signal to the men to hold their fire to avoid hitting Dr. Ryan.

"You have come to your death," Tamir-Benob said as he managed to fire a couple of rounds with the firestick, he had taken with him.

"Take cover!" yelled Rodriguez, but two team members were already wounded. A Crow tribe member, who was trying to sneak up on the giant was caught and speared for efforts.

Tamir-Benob continued through the formation carrying Ryan toward the entrance.

"Face me you coward," Jim Blackhawk yelled, charging at the creature. He swung a big knife, but Tamir-Benob grabbed his wrist and forced him to the ground and jerked the knife away.

"You dare challenge me?" Tamir-Benob raged, delivering a knee hard to Jim Blackhawk's ribs. The sound of cracking bones echoed against the cave walls. The giant threw Ryan down and locked eyes with Whitman before turning toward Blackhawk again.

"No, don't do it, fight me!" Whitman yelled.

"Watch, Ironhorse, as I take your friend's life," Tamir-Benob said, his voice deep and evil. He plunged the blade of Blackhawk's own knife into his heart. Blackhawk looked up briefly, and then slumped over, devoid of life.

"No, you monster!" shrieked Whitman.

Tears streamed down Ryan's face. This nightmare would never end.

Tamir-Benob turned and pick up his sword and Dr. Ryan, then made his way toward the cave entrance. Whitman and the Ranger team followed.

General Briggs watched via satellite imagery as the giant exited the cave. Was it time to intervene? He could deploy missiles from the drones and end this now. There would be collateral damage, but it would be over. Mass casualties were not ideal, especially friendly casualties at the hand of US military drones. Perhaps the soldiers would prevail with just a bit more time. His partners wouldn't like this turn of events, but Briggs felt they could still control the situation if they had satellite imagery and an active drone.

"Rodriguez, we have one last chance before he escapes. I'll take the last IA man with me and catch the beast about two hundred yards from here in the clearing. You need to push him toward us. We'll surprise him, and I'll end this," Whitman confirmed.

"Not sure this will work, but General Briggs is on board for now. If you don't take him out, we'll call in the drones before he gets away. Got it?"

Whitman left with his man to cut the creature off, but it was difficult to focus, as he was fighting the emotion of seeing Blackhawk murdered in front of his eyes. They were taking a short cut to end up near the edge of a drop-off and cliff.

Tamir-Benob noticed the soldiers following as he left the cave. The trail went upward toward the mountain peaks. It had stopped raining, providing a small reprieve. He was badly injured and needed time to heal. The only way he would recover would be consumption of heavy protein. The woman's constant kicking and squirming was slowing his progress.

"Be quiet and stop kicking or I will kill you now and be done with it," he ordered as he slapped her across the face, turning her cheek red.

Ryan reached up in return and scratched him across his bearded cheek, drawing blood. He was about to strike her again when he saw movement from the soldiers. He refocused his attention on moving forward.

Whitman and the last IA tribesman ran ahead to the ambush sight, hoping to arrive before the giant.

"Hurry, every second is critical," Whitman whispered.

Rodriguez needed to slow the beast down. "Take the shot," he ordered his sniper.

The sniper managed to hit the giant in a leg, eliciting a curse, but doing little to slow him down.

"General, we're taking one last shot at stopping this thing. Confirming if the drones are ready to call if we need them," asked Rodriguez?

Tamir-Benob heard the voices of the soldiers and ran faster to avoid capture. Ryan kicked at the creature to no avail as they moved up the mountain slope.

>>>> <<<<

Whitman and his companion silently made it to the rendezvous site near the cliff. The drop-off was over a thousand feet. There was shrubbery, small trees, and rocks available for concealment. They had few weapons at this point and would need the military's help. After using leaves to wipe their tracks from the dirt, they took their position up wind and waited.

"Rodriguez, this is Whitman over."

"Go ahead."

"We're in place and will engage when possible."

"We're trailing, and about five minutes behind. He should be arriving in the next one to two minutes. Good luck."

Whitman turned to his comrade. "Stary sharp. He'll be here in the next minute." He said silent prayers to the Great Spirit and waited for the inevitable.

The giant approached and put Ryan down hard, stopping to catch his breath. *A good place for an ambush.* He smelled the scent of the soldiers trailing, but there was no sign of Ironhorse. That was troubling, and he would need to be on the lookout for a trap.

A twig snapped ahead, startling him. He turned to see Ironhorse and another warrior about to use their firestick. The bullets burned his chest, and the pain made him fall onto his back.

"Now's our chance, let's go!" Whitman yelled. Throwing down the spent rifles, both Crow warriors ran toward the struggling giant.

Whitman went airborne and flew headlong into Tamir-Benob, keeping the beast from standing up. Ryan backed away from the scuffle to keep from getting pulled in. Whitman thrust his military-grade knife into his nemesis over and over. The bloodied giant pushed Whitman off as the second warrior blazed in for an attack. Tamir-Benob snatched the second attacker and put him in a choke hold with his massive arm.

"No!" yelled Whitman as the giant snapped the neck of his fellow tribesman.

Tamir-Benob pushed the warrior's motionless body to the side and stood up. He grabbed his sword and turned his attention to Whitman. "Time to finish this. Your time is up, and the other soldiers will follow."

Still trying to catch his breath, Whitman replied coldly, "You are the only one left who's dying on this mountain today, you bastard."

Ryan silently picked up a sizeable stick and faced the giant head-on. She had no fear, only rage in her eyes. The hybrid looked her way, surprised. "I should have killed you earlier. You are more trouble than you are worth."

Whitman was out of ammo, but he stood and circled around the giant slowly with his knife ready for battle. The giant held his sword in one hand. Whitman was outmatched and didn't have an attack angle.

Laughing arrogantly, the red-haired beast stuck his sword in the dirt and waved for Whitman to come closer. "I will give you a chance, just like Goliath gave David. Although there will be a different outcome this time."

Before Whitman could move, Ryan sprinted forward and swung her makeshift sword, breaking it over the giant's legs. She had managed to irritate him but nothing more. He was swinging wildly at her now. She scooped up a fistful of gravel and sand as she ducked to avoid the reach of his long arms. She tossed the dirt in his eyes, momentarily blinding him.

The giant cursed at her, giving Whitman the opening, he needed. He sprinted forward and jumped onto Tamir-Benob's back, intent on cutting the giant's jugular. Whitman wasn't quite fast enough and Tamir-Benob blocked the knife. The result was a mere flesh wound, giving the giant the upper hand. With his free hand, Tamir-Benob reached behind him and slung Whitman off his back.

"This is only prolonging both of your deaths. You cannot beat me," he said.

Whitman slowly got up as the giant walked toward him. He had picked up his knife while repositioning himself for the attack. His only chance to get needed space was to use a little judo and the giant's momentum against him. Ryan cringed as she watched the fight. There must be something else she could do.

Tamir-Benob confidently lumbered toward Whitman, who grabbed the giant's wrist and used forward momentum to throw him down. Whitman grabbed Ryan's hand and sprinted away. Enraged, Tamir-Benob stood up and started to chase them.

"Down on your knees or we shoot," shouted Rodriguez as the Ranger team came into the clearing.

Before the soldiers could react, Tamir-Benob threw his small knife. The nearest Ranger fell over clutching his chest. The team quickly opened heavy fire in response. Smoke filled the air from the gunfire.

Tamir-Benob fell over, blood streaming out of the barrage of bullet wounds. His body was unable to heal. He had lost too much blood in a short period of time. He drew on a hidden strength and with one last effort reached out with his sword and slashed another soldier, cutting into the man's stomach as he tried to dodge.

"Stop him!" an angry Rodriguez ordered as the giant caught his rifle and forced it up. Multiple rounds shot into the air. An injured giant ripped the rifle away and used it as a club trying to knock the team lead unconscious. Rodriguez partially deflected the blow to his head at the last minute.

Tamir-Benob withdrew the knife from a nearby slain soldier and approached the two remaining team members. Both raised their rifles and continued firing, but the giant threw the bloodied knife, hitting one soldier in the neck.

The last soldier held his ground, unleashing a shower of bullets upon the giant. Tamir-Benob grabbed his sword. Using it to deflect some of the bullets raining down on him, he advanced on the remaining soldier with a look of pure evil and skewered him.

Only Whitman and Ryan remained now. It was time to end this.

"Frank, no!" Ryan screamed, but Whitman was already on the move.

The giant let out a roar of pain as Whitman plunged his knife into Tamir-Benob's back just below his shoulder. Tamir-Benob struggled to reach the knife protruding from his back.

"You will get your death today," Whitman yelled in the giant's ear as he backed closer to the edge of the cliff. He took out his Tomahawk, razor-sharp.

"Do you think that you can kill me with that tiny ax when nothing else has worked?"

"You underestimate your opponents, just like your forefathers. Is this why your kind was defeated by man? By the future king of Israel? No humanity, only death and destruction. You could work with us, seek to do good. You're pathetic."

"Do not mock me. The child had help from his Hebrew God. But you are alone, warrior!"

"And what if I have help from the Great Spirit?"

"There is no Great Spirit, only the cursed Hebrew God. After being here on this wretched earth for thousands of years, that I know."

"I need no god, beast. Just the steel and strength of my right arm and the determination to end you." Whitman needed to time his move exactly to position the giant over the edge. Ryan saw what Whitman was doing and crept closer to try and help.

The giant continued toward the edge, then paused and threw his sword down. "I would rather use my bare hands to strangle the life from your body."

"So be it, but it will be your final mistake," Whitman muttered. He sprinted at the beast with tomahawk in hand. Tamir-Benob caught Whitman in midair, but he still landed several hurtful blows to Tamir-Benob's chest. The lacerations bled badly, and the giant was wobbly now and dropped Whitman. They were face-to-face and Whitman had managed to maneuver the monster near the edge of the cliff.

That was the opening Ryan needed to make her move. She picked up a rifle and ran straight at the giant.

He saw her coming and took his eyes off Whitman. "I see you, woman. Do you think to sneak up on me?"

"See this you monster," yelled Ryan as she pulled the trigger and shot him over and over. His shoulders smoked from the gunshots. He kicked at her but missed. She dashed back out of his reach with only adrenaline driving her.

Whitman ran and jumped at the giant again, but wound up suspended in midair by his shirt, tightly in the giant's grasp. Tamir-Benob pulled Whitman close until they were face-to-face once again. Whitman could smell the beast's rotten breath, see his canine incisors, feel his rough red beard against his skin.

"So here we are, warrior. You are about to take your last breath. Never has one fought like this. You have lasted longer than your ancestors."

"I intend to last longer than you, monster. I brought something special for you!" Whitman slammed his tomahawk into Tamir-Benob's forehead. He dropped Whitman and fell back. As he stumbled and tried to regain his balance, Tamir-Benob slipped off the edge of the cliff and disappeared from sight.

Ryan and Whitman looked on in disbelief.

"Is this nightmare finally over?" Ryan asked.

"I'm not sure. Surely a fall like that would kill him," Whitman said, shaking his head from the shock of it all.

"This still doesn't seem real," Ryan replied. They paused, hoping it was over.

They were in disbelief as two large hands appeared on the edge of the cliff. The giant must have caught a rock on the way down and then climbed back up.

Whitman struggled to pick up Tamir-Benob's enormous sword just as an evil head with orange eyes and red beard showed itself.

"You have not killed me warrior, only slowed me."

"You are wrong, foul creature of the fallen. Just like David wounded your ancestor Goliath and then took his head, I do the same." With a swift move Whitman ran up and swung the sword, still sharp after all this time. He took a certain satisfaction from cutting his enemy's head off with his own sword.

Tamir-Benob's head rolled onto the edge with eyes open and an evil frown still on his face. His headless body fell from the cliff, landing a thousand feet below on the forest floor.

"Now it's over, Kathryn."

Ryan stood motionless for a long time, just waiting for something else to happen. Finally, she asked, "What do we do now?"

"Let's burn his head, and then we'll see if any of the soldiers survived. We have a lot of things to take care of, and people to talk to."

Ryan turned and buried her face in Whitman's chest. He held her as she let all the emotions she'd been holding in escape through her tears.

"Thank you for being there," she said.

"You did pretty good on your own."

"I'm definitely looking forward to that glass of wine later." She felt safe for the first time in days and thrilled that they were getting out of the forest.

They could hear the sound of the helicopters approaching. After placing dry leavers near the monstrous severed head, Whitman quickly lit a fire. As the fire burned, they walked over to check for survivors.

Rodriguez was alive but moving slowly, a likely concussion. Whitman helped the wounded soldier up. He and the sniper were the only survivors of the group. The helicopter managed to land nearby, and a team of soldiers quickly secured the area.

"Is that what I think it is?" Rodriguez said, looking at the head burning a few feet away.

"Yep. The rest of him went over the edge of the cliff," Whitman said tiredly.

Before boarding the helicopter, Whitman alerted the Crow tribal headquarters to look for the dead giant's body at the base of the cliff. He wasn't sure if they would find it before the military, but they had to try.

# Chapter Twenty-Four
# Survivors Tale

IT HAD BEEN SEVERAL weeks since the final confrontation with Tamir-Benob. Everything Whitman had experienced on that cold mountain still seemed unbelievable. Sleep only came in few hour bits, as the face of the behemoth haunted him. He was slowly recovering from his physical wounds and had spent a lot of time with his daughter appreciating their moments together.

"Dad, are you ready to go?

"Yes, Katrina, let's head out." They were headed for their favorite restaurant. His worldview had changed, and there was much to contemplate, including thoughts on the spiritual realm.

Perhaps he should have listened more to his tribal legends, but that still would not have prepared him for this encounter. He now understood that there were more unknowns in the world than he'd realized before and that absolute evil really did exist. Being able to protect his family and friends was now a paramount priority, but how to do that was the question.

This nightmare had resulted in the death of fourteen Crow warriors, including tribal elder Mighty Eagle and his dear friend Jim Blackhawk. The feeling of loss was overwhelming. Mighty Eagle had children, and Whitman tried to spend time consoling them, but they were still in shock. There were twice as many soldiers killed in the process.

Working to restore normalcy to the tribe and its people would take a long time. There were so many questions. Only those closest to him knew the truth, but even they were still in disbelief. Their tribal legends had been true, and since the caves were on tribal land, their people had at least been able to take pictures of the artwork and maintain some control.

The federal government had insisted on blocking the entrance to the cave that contained artifacts for national security. The governor was still livid over the matter, but his options were limited. The cover story reported to the public through the media was an experiment gone wrong involving soldiers who reacted badly to investigational drugs. The number of deaths had been underreported on purpose and were falsified to be linked to other events, such as training activities. Families were compensated to avoid lawsuits. Those involved signed nondisclosures, but word would eventually leak out. Rumors about creatures in the mountains on the internet had already started.

Although the military had contained the situation, a few religious groups had asked questions to members of the tribe. It was no surprise to hear from the Vatican, but a few other groups unknown to Whitman had also inquired. The details these groups had obtained was impressive given the control of information. Perhaps there were legitimate groups out there who tracked these types of creatures and understood the risk to mankind.

There was no mention of the outside extraction team who took Mullins. It must have been embarrassing to the military, and they would be pursuing him. It had turned out Mullins had a history of extremist religious beliefs, but no one in his immediate circle had been aware how deep these beliefs went and to the extent they affected him. It was a scary thought what he could do with the knowledge he had if provided the right lab setting. At least Whitman could let federal agents worry about him.

The burials of his fellow tribesman had been completed, and it was time to replace the brave men from Indian Affairs who had been lost. Not an easy task, but life went on, and the people needed a robust police force.

Since the military had monitored everything by satellite, they knew the giant had fallen down the cliff. Although IA had tried to get there first, the military was able to obtain the giant's body before tribal members could. At least the giant was dead when the military took him, so at most they would have DNA.

The giant had told them that a cloned body would be susceptible to hosting a dead spirit of his kind. Whitman had hoped this wasn't true, and he couldn't imagine the havoc another one of these beasts could impart, let alone if there were more than one running around. If there were others of Tamir-Benob's kind out there, Whitman prayed he would never come across one again. He wanted to find an expert on the matter and inquire. He had found a name to follow up with.

The military compound near the reservation border had been closed, probably permanently.

After dinner with his daughter, Whitman spoke to Ryan. "How is it going?"

"Keeping me busy since the transfer to the new posting," she said.

"Are we still planning that Italian dinner?"

"You bet. I have a few days off coming up."

The military had promoted Ryan and moved her back to their main DEVCOM facility in the Boston area. She either didn't know or couldn't talk about what happened to the Nephilim's body and DNA sample. Whitman suspected the project would move to another secret military lab without Ryan but couldn't verify.

Whitman had also reached out to Stone's family. He felt bad how things went down for Stone, and he was saddened that the family would never know the truth behind his death. Stone exemplified the Ranger credo, and outside of this crazy situation they could have been friends. The secrecy behind all this was disheartening. It was a lot for him to take in and contemplate going forward.

⫸⫷

General Briggs had been in damage control mode after the incident. The Pentagon had him on a short leash, and folks were shocked when he resigned.

The giant's body had been sent to a secret underground facility out west among other classified projects. The DNA went to three facilities for study and use for military applications. It would take the military years to move from concept to useability. Before Briggs's departure, a special reconnaissance program in the Middle East had been started. If there was one of the Nephilim's kind, there might be a second one. The military had learned from this experience and would be better prepared when and if they had a second capture.

Although the applications were profound, military leaders were concerned about the existence of more of these creatures and what would happen if they decided to insert their influence. There were minimal things the military could do now without alerting the public and causing massive casualties if they had to engage these creatures in the future. The president was briefed and wanted more options in dealing with these creatures, given what they found in the writing of the parchments.

Somewhere near Jackson Whole, Wyoming, Briggs was enjoying his civilian career. He looked out the window of his luxury cabin at the snowy mountain tops. He paced in front of his fireplace and blew smoke from a fresh Cuban cigar.

"Gentlemen, given the circumstances we have implemented our contingency plan. Multiple teams are on the ground in the Middle East following up on leads on more of these creatures. Our monitoring programs have picked up activity from the CIA and the Vatican, amongst others, as their interest has ramped up as well. If they find something, we'll intervene. Our surveillance has also identified an unknown private group in Europe, but we are early in the assessment of their abilities," Briggs said.

"What are the chances one of these players is ahead of us?" an unnamed associate asked.

"If the European group has Mullins and a sample, which we assume someone does, they're ahead of us. We have multiple teams looking for him. There is less of a chance he is with a rogue nation, as I think he would find that less appealing. When he's found, we'll try to acquire him and any of his existing work. That should ensure we stay ahead of the competition. If we can't extract him, he will be sanctioned."

Far away in a remote part of Western Europe, Mullins finished his cappuccino while reviewing the day's test results. The taste of real Italian roast coffee with brioche was so much more relaxing than in the States. He had adjusted to his new life, and mission easily.

His team had spent the last two weeks sequencing DNA from the giant and running simulations. The preliminary results were unbelievable. Genes that were not present in the human genome and additional existing genes with greater expression were identified. This could help explain some of the incredible attributes the creature had exhibited and possibly lead to insertion and expression in human subjects.

"Dr. Schmidt, the others are here for the weekly meeting," Gunther reminded him.

"I'll be right there, Gunther." He grabbed his notes and stood up to go meet with the visitors in the conference area. He paused momentarily near his Crosby record player. Security at the compound had increased, but he was enjoying his frequent visits to the countryside. Soldiers still followed him on his strolls, but from a distance.

The council was pleased with the early results and pressed him to explore early experimentation with humans as soon as possible. Van Wilhelm had provided more reading material on Nephilim origins taken from various Church archives and recent reports of activities in other parts of the world where there may be Nephilim presence.

Mullins smiled in anticipation of what was to come as he turned off the Mozart playing softly in the background. So much to do, and so little time.

# Notes From the Author

**A** s **a first-time novelist**, I would like to share the basis for the current story. My goal was to build a believable story focusing on the tales of large humanlike hybrid giants, while blending aspects of religion, archaeology, and military science.

Discussion of physical giants has been ongoing in many cultures for thousands of years. In researching this topic, I found over fifty cultures that described humanoid like giants in their civilizations or who had significant writings in their history on this topic. Granted, much of the source material available is questionable in accuracy or in some circumstances based on speculation. It is also impossible in most references to distinguish from true giants and those individuals who simply appeared larger than normal for that time period and were termed "giants."

My research so far suggests that reliable historical evidence is rarely available to the public at large. However, with so much anecdotal and secondhand information written on the topic in various cultures, these tales must contain some nuggets of truth.

When penning the *Genesis 6 Project* story line, I started with two initial questions to guide the story: Would it even be possible that giants existed in the past, and under what conditions could they exist today?

To keep things less complicated, my research focus for the story was limited to the last few thousand years. Most discussions described physical giants with a height range of ten-to-fifteen feet, with most having above average strength, and without medical conditions such as acromegaly.

Some commentators will rightfully point out that it is impossible to obtain such a height, given the stresses placed on bones and the probability of collapse under body weight. I am aware of the square cube law proposed by Galileo, which says that as a shape grows, its volume grows faster than its surface area. At face value, if you apply this law to modern man, then a physical giant seems impractical. But I will explain my logic on why that maybe in error momentarily.

Before speculating, let's first look at human normal maximums. The tallest human on record, Robert Wadlow was eight feet eleven inches. There are also a handful of people in the world today or in the past standing above eight feet tall.

Although very tall and weighing over four hundred pounds at his maximal weight, Mr. Wadlow suffered from many health conditions and walked with a cane. It is highly likely that normal human development has genetic and physical limits, which is why we rarely see individuals over eight feet tall, and if so with many health ailments.

Continuing with this line of reasoning, if giants of old existed (considering the limits to the square cube law), their genetic stock would have to be different than that of today's typical humans. That hypothetical and unproven difference serves as a foundation for this story.

If we take our thinking a step further and surmise that fallen angels or spiritual entities left their home in a biblical sense (heaven) on more than one occasion and, when entering our domain, had the ability to take on human form, then we have a basis for this story. Considerably, this is a big leap in logic, and many will consider it unbelievable. That is ok, as I am simply trying to weave a tale of possibilities.

The debate as to whether incorporeal angels exist or have human bodies is beyond the scope here, but excellent commentary on the topic has been written by Dr. Michael Heiser and Gary Wayne. Although there are numerous stories in biblical literature where this did occur (i.e., angels with Lot during Sodom and Gomorra, etc.).

If fallen angels or other spiritual entities with the ability to take on humanoid bodies existed in the past, or even in a make-believe fashion, it is probable they would also have different genetic makeup. Any offspring from these entities most likely would also have a different genetic makeup than average humans if we assume their offspring inherited some of the father's genes. Granted, these are big leaps in logic!

Different genes or gene expression from a superior being could easily manifest as different body sizes, greater strength, and characteristics like more dense bone mineral content and greater explosive muscle fibre than the average human. Interestingly there have been isolated cases where humans have been born with extremely high bone density from increased activity of the gene LRP5, for example.

We have also seen studies that in athletes and animals there can be variations in myostatin gene activity resulting in increased levels of strength and muscularity. So, this suggests that if enough human genes were up or down regulated, people could appear superhuman and demonstrate performance attributes above human expectations. So, the concept of a supernatural human-looking being with different genetic makeup may not be as far-fetched as it sounds. Hence, the square cube law may not be completely rate limiting depending on genetic activity.

In researching this story, some early source material included the biblical and non-biblical books of Genesis, Jubilees, Giants, and Enoch. Other interesting reads included *The Works of Flavius Josephus*, Pigafetta's diary with the Patagonian giants, the historian Augustus on Emperor Maximinus Thrax, and others. In both biblical canonical and noncanonical books, there are astounding tales.

I made a personal unsubstantiated interpretation that a second incursion of fallen angels occurred after the great flood described in the time period of the Bible. This itself is a controversial topic, and many will argue there is little basis for this. A second incursion of fallen angels mating with humans would have allowed the creation of giants, and their subsequent children the Nephilim. Again, many will challenge the merits of this assumption.

In my thought process, and that of many others before me, if these hybrid creatures truly existed, they could have easily masqueraded as some of the Greek, Norse, and other mythology gods and demigods in history.

Many will argue it is not biologically possible for these hybrid humans to exist for many reasons as described above. If evaluating with today's science, that is a reasonable argument. As a trained researcher, I would argue that biological tools, knowledge of the past, and spiritual acumen are not advanced enough today to address all these questions adequately. Unless hidden away by governments or clandestine groups, these types of creatures don't seem to exist in our modern times. But who is to say that hybrid genetic makeups were not possible years ago? What if there was greater spiritual or supernatural activity many years ago, but less today as society evolved and lost belief? What about countless examples of animals and plants today that were much larger many years ago? How is that possible and explainable? I would like to point out that man has more questions unanswered about our existence and spirituality than we have answers for. We shouldn't be so quick to rule out things we don't believe or understand right away.

Another event that helps seed this book was the unsubstantiated rumor that the US military fought and killed a twelve-foot giant with red hair in the remote mountains of Kandahar in the early 2000s. There have been multiple internet rumors of sightings of these type of creatures in the Wakhan Corridor, but again nothing of substantial proof. Some have claimed to have been witnesses, but it is difficult to confirm. I would not expect the US military to admit these sightings or any interactions, if they did occur, to the public for several reasons. Could we imagine the pandemonium and impact on society, including religion, if this was reported? A sudden worldview that something more powerful than man existed on the earth would be a foundational shift.

The hybrid creature in this Genesis 6 tale was made to be the grandson of an immensely powerful fallen angel from the time of King David of the biblical telling, hence his unusually long-life span and ability to recover quickly from mortal man's weapons. The current story blends the biblical narrative with the Kandahar claims.

For a moment, let's assume something like this did occur, and instead of killing the Nephilim creature, he had been brought to a secret US research facility for genetic testing and eventual gene transfer to human test subjects. This is not too far-fetched.

I am assuming the US military certainly has secret weapons programs, and most likely many unexplained things under research. Would the US government be involved in research related to nonhuman genetics? Your guess is as good as mine.

However, the concept of genetic manipulation is controversial and has the potential to become prominent in the coming years. Some of these technologies are known to me, and the possibilities of genetically altering humans is frightening and borders on unethical. Unfortunately, there will be bad actors on the world stage who will ultimately attempt or who are already manipulating genes for nefarious purposes.

In real life, the US military DEVCOM group portrayed in the story is charged with developing soldier capabilities for combat. I hold a lot of respect for our men and women in uniform. There is a lot of work going on with the Department of Defense DARPA group (exoskeletons, cyborg implants, etc.) and most likely other non-DARPA secret programs to help US soldiers. There are many good people working with honorable ideas, protecting our troops, and in no way was this story portrayal intended to be derogatory. Although in the story there is another group on the board, guiding the fictional General Briggs on decisions. They make their presence known, and in the future will have a bigger influence in events.

The made-up Billings, Montana, military research laboratory is near the Crow Indian Reservation. The town of Pryor and the Pryor Mountains are actual locations close to Billings. There are many caves as described in the story with lots of forest area. Given the rich history that American Indians bring to the United States, my desire was to make the fictional hero of the story a member of the Apsáalooke Crow Nation. There is also a strong history in Native American lore related to interactions with giants. I tried to be as accurate as possible, although there may be some unintentional inaccuracies.

The Council of Five is entirely fictional. The idea was to identify a group of wealthy, successful power brokers who manipulate world events. Some speculate there are secret groups like this, possibly with a religious bent, who manipulate events for personal gain and power. There are probably groups who have in the past tried to influence world events (the Illuminati, Bilderberg, etc.), but again it is not clear to what extent, and if they have explored supernatural means to help accomplish this.

One might ask what is next, and if this would turn into a series. I don't know just yet. Ironhorse will be taking a break for now but could return for a future story. There are lots of ideas for a second book. Dr. Mullins is now involved in a flurry of activity and may show his evil and conniving ways again. We can certainly expect the Council of Five to insert their influence on the world stage. Who knows, maybe we will see the Vatican or other supernatural influencers in the next round. What if there were other figures from the Nephilim world? Perhaps a story including the great King Og, or even the might warrior Nimrod.

Could the spirit being one of these dead Nephilim possess a mortal body? Lots of possibilities, so stay tuned. I am just getting started!

Michael Ferguson

# About Author

Michael Ferguson has always had an interest in science fiction, including the supernatural. After reading hundreds of great novels, he decided to put his own ideas to paper. He and his wife enjoy traveling in their spare time, listening to classical jazz and looking forward to reviews of his first book. Please post your thoughts at Amazon!

Ingram Content Group UK Ltd.
Milton Keynes UK
UKHW022016200423
420514UK00010B/671